Something in the Shadows
A Halloween Anthology

Melanie Gilbert

Christis Christie

Heather Karn

Elle Beaumont

A Halloween Anthology

Something in the Shadows

With stories by:
Christis Christie, Elle Beaumont,
Heather Karn, Melanie Gilbert

For those who love all things dark and beautiful.

Headless

Melanie Gilbert

1

"In a quarter mile, your destination will be on the left." The monotone GPS' voice gave both me and my bladder hope. Maybe I wouldn't wet my pants after all.

The lodge for Ranger's Ranch came into view and I took the turn into the gravel drive a little faster than I should have. That didn't stop me from speeding up the long road to the lodge's parking area. Dust washed over the car as I came to an abrupt halt between a black SUV and my bestie's yellow Range Rover. Was I still jealous of her car six months after she'd bought it while I drove something a step above a beater? Yes.

Other cars filled the parking area, but my bladder screamed to find a bathroom so loud that I didn't care to look around. If anyone else I knew had arrived, I'd see them inside instead of searching the lot for their car.

My phone rang as I turned off the car's ignition. The sound of Justin Timberlake's voice singing the tune of "Sexy-Back" made me yip and dive into the purse beside me before anyone could possibly hear the ringtone I did not choose. I'd picked a classy Harry Potter theme, but my sister thought that too tame. Now I regretted my lack of password on the phone during my visit home last weekend.

The phone showed my sister's face. Being the awesome

sister who had to pee that I was, I ignored the call and promptly changed the call volume to vibrate before dropping the phone back into my purse.

Grabbing my purse off the seat, I shoved my door open. "Ouch!"

Dang it, I'd hit someone. I bit down on my lower lip as I looked up into the face of a god. I winced. Of all the men on Earth, I'd hit the district manager with my car door. Not only was he the god of hot men with his sandy brown hair, brilliant blue eyes that dazzled in pictures, and broad shoulders, but he was also my boss' boss and son of the company's president, Henry Simmons.

"Sorry, Mr. Simmons."

"Could you close your door so I can close mine?" He grabbed something off the passenger seat of his SUV and waited for me to get my head together to close my door.

My cheeks would have lit a forest on fire as I closed my car door, much to the objection of my bladder. I should have stopped alongside the road. No one would have seen me relieve my poor bladder in a stand of trees ten miles back, but I'd allowed pride to make me miserable.

The cell phone in my purse buzzed as Bryce Simmons closed his door and walked to the lodge. This time, my BFF's face showed on the screen.

"Hey, Zoe, can I call you back?"

"Eloise, are you here yet, girl?" I shouldn't have answered the phone because Zoe would never listen to an attempt to call her back.

"Yes." I groaned as Bryce Simmons and his tight backside entered the building.

"What is it? Where are you? I have our room key."

"I smacked Bryce Simmons with my car door. Hard." I dropped my forehead to my steering wheel as the reality of what I'd done fully sunk in.

"You did what?" Zoe's shriek broke my eardrum before I could pull my phone from my ear.

"I have to pee. I'll call you back." I hung up on her, something I'd hear about later, but there was no time to care now.

After checking to make sure my door wouldn't hit anymore hunks, I opened the door and climbed awkwardly to my feet. My walk up the stairs and into the building was an incredibly sexy waddle from full bladder and stiff legs. I'd been on the road for ten hours. Normally I'd tell someone to bug off if they mentioned how nice I walked, but as the sun began to set behind the horizon, I was all for keeping my mouth shut. I was too tired. They could think what they wanted.

The lobby of the place was amazing, just as it had been last year. The natural, smoothed wood accents were comforting against the Halloween decorations of orange and black. Even a large pine tree stood in a corner beside a burning fireplace with its orange lights and pumpkin garland creating the mood in the room. Halloween had been, and always would be, my least favorite holiday of the year. Still, Ranger's Ranch knew how to decorate.

A hallway at the back of the room held a family bathroom. I made a beeline straight there. The motion sensor witch that sprang to life and cackled at me from her bench beside the hallway nearly created a puddle on the floor.

"Of all the nonsensical decorations to put by a bathroom." No one was around to hear my muttered grievance, so I kept walking.

At the door to the bathroom, I pushed down on the handle. It didn't swing down to open the door. Locked.

I rapped on the door hard and fast. "Is there anyone in there?"

No one spoke, or at least I didn't hear them over the music playing from an overhead speaker, so I rapped harder and faster. "Hello? If there's someone in there, please say something so I know the toilet's not broken."

An employee passed the opening of the hallway, heading further into the main lobby area, and I rushed to catch him.

"Excuse me-ahh!" The witch sensor caught me, again, and she cackled while I nearly wet myself, again, and gave the employee a heart attack because of my scream.

"Can I help you?" The young man was kind enough not to mention my near murder of him.

"I'm so sorry. Can you tell me if there's something wrong with the bathroom?" I pointed over my shoulder to the hallway.

"Um, I don't think so, but I can go check?" He didn't want to, but I nodded, and he was off to the front desk.

While he was gone, I made my way back to the bathroom door, prepared for Miss Cackle this time around, and gave a long series of knocks on the door. Still no answer and I'd even put my ear to the wood to really listen hard this time.

I turned my back on the door, leaning against it while waiting for the young man to return to inform me the bathroom was out of service.

"Apparently this is your lucky day, Eloise." After ten hours by myself, and being a naturally chatty soul, I'd taken to talking to myself to fill the silence when music and audiobooks had grown old in the car.

The door behind me flew open. I, of course, went with it.

"Ahh!" My arms pinwheeled to catch my balance, but I still fell backwards.

Strong arms caught me before my butt or head hit the ground. I did manage to hit my rescuer with my flailing, for which I felt bad, but they were kind enough to put me back on my feet anyway.

"Oh my gosh, thank you." I held a hand to my chest as I turned with a smile upon my rescuer. "You saved my-"

Bryce Simmons, god of all gods, stood looking down on me with mild annoyance written in every line of his face. I cringed.

"Sorry? Again?"

I backed out of the bathroom as the young employee, announced by mechanic cackles, strode down the hallway.

"There's nothing wrong with the bathroom." He paused with a smile as Mr. Simmons exited the room. "But I guess you can see that."

"Yeah, thanks." I gave the lodge's employee a halfhearted, wimpy salute and he was on his way with laughter that I'd been the cause of creating.

Bryce, otherwise known to Zoe and I as Simmering Simmons because of his obvious hotness, glanced down his nose at me.

"I did respond to you by the way. The door is thick and the music up there," he pointed to the ceiling speaker, "is very loud."

"Oh."

We stood in awkward silence while my bladder screamed.

"Well, um…" What in the world did I say to get out of this?

"Where are you heading next, Ms..." Bryce raised an eyebrow when I didn't give my name on schedule.

"Brandt. I'm Eloise Brandt, sir."

"You know me, so I assume you work for the company?"

My cheeks heated so much they nearly burned. "Yeah, I do. Norman Gates is my boss."

He nodded. "I see. Well, is this," he waved a hand between us, "going to keep happening? I just need to know if I should wear armor or be on the lookout."

"No, sir. I'll watch out better. I just really need to use the bathroom. For like, twenty miles." This was the most embarrassing moment of my life and I was having it in front of Simmering Simmons. Zoe would kill me for this! She'd keep a mile from me while at the retreat.

Bryce stepped aside and motioned to the bathroom. "All yours. Enjoy your evening."

I didn't allow him time to walk away before I ran into the bathroom and pretty much slammed the door behind me. I made sure to lock it straightway so no crazy person who needed to pee as badly as I did would barge in on me.

After taking care of business, for which my bladder was so happy, I stared at myself in the mirror while the water ran down the sink.

"Eloise, you are in so much trouble. So much. Don't count on a promotion. Just look for a new job. It'll be easier and less embarrassing for you in years to come." My shoulders fell and my reflection pouted. I really liked my job.

I grabbed my phone out of my purse when I left the bathroom and scowled at the witch when she cackled at me as I entered the lobby where people from my office and other areas gathered to meet up with each other.

"Where are you?" Zoe answered the phone in a tizzy. "I can't see you – wait there you are."

Zoe, with her black hair in tight curls, bounced down the stairs of the lodge. Her jeans were tight as was her shirt, regular Zoe style, but she had the body for it. Me, not so much.

"Eloise, what in the world is this?" Zoe waved her arms up and down at my appearance. Wrinkled shirt and what she called "last season's holey jeans" were my travel apparel. Ten hours in a car meant I'd wanted to be comfortable. Meeting Simmering Simmons hadn't been on my list of things to do with sparse makeup, a crooked ponytail, and my current garb. Neither had smacking him with my door or falling on him in the bathroom been on the agenda.

To save my ego, I gave Zoe a half-hearted glare as I turned to leave the building, my bestie at my side. "Unlike you, Zo, I had to drive the entire ten hours today, not start yesterday and sleep over at family's house halfway."

"You could have come with me."

"That would have been weird, and I had to drop Mr. Muffin Top at the sitter's last night after work." The cat didn't like me much and preferred the sitter so that had gone smoothly.

"And you hadn't finished packing because you're the world's biggest procrastinator. Not to mention you bring the weirdest stuff with you on trips. And, you don't use a list so you're running around last-minute packing stuff."

Zoe shook her head at me when I popped the trunk.

"What?" I looked into the trunk.

"Girl, no one else brings a sword on a company retreat."

"We're in the middle of nowhere. Anything could happen.

Besides, Dad gave it to me last weekend when I was at their place and I forgot to take it upstairs."

"Sure, ya did. More like conveniently left it inside the trunk for a week." Well, she wasn't wrong. "Okay, let's grab these bags, leave the sword, and go upstairs and you can tell me about what happened with Simmer and how much damage control we'll have to run."

Zoe stopped walking when I didn't leave the back of the car, hand over my eyes. She groaned.

"It's that bad? Please tell me it's not. I mean, you hit him with your car door. Right? Can't be all that bad. He didn't fire you."

I peeked at her between my fingers. "It got worse."

She gaped at me. "Do I even want to know?"

"Probably not."

Her shoulders fell. "Come on. Let's get upstairs so you can tell me whatever horrific thing I need to know about, and I then I can proceed with the lecture."

My bestie turned and began walking up the stairs to the lodge while I followed. Well, at least she'd taken things well so far. I had a bestie for about maybe a half an hour longer. Then all bets were off.

2

"Please, tell me this isn't happening." Zoe laid on her bed with an arm slung over her face, hiding from my bad news.

"You think it's bad for you? What about me?" My reflection in the room's large mirror made me wince.

Zoe had been right. The tiny bathroom mirror down in the hallway off the lobby hadn't shown how rough I looked. Now, I had my appearance to add to my growing list of embarrassments.

"We grab our schedules at breakfast tomorrow. Maybe you and I will be lucky enough not to be in the same group for activities."

I gave Zoe the stink eye for her comment.

"What?" She sat up and threw her legs off the bed. "You're the one who did this, not me. Now, are you hungry because I'm starving."

"Yes."

"Okay, go change." Zoe tipped her head to indicate the bathroom. "It's a very nice bathroom."

"I was here last year, Zo. I know." My shoulders sagged and I let out a deep breath. "Sorry, Zo. It's been a long day.

I'm tired, hungry, and embarrassed. Maybe you should head downstairs, and I'll meet you down there."

"Nope. Not happening." Zoe shook her head back and forth. "You were alone too much today and that led to simmering amounts of trouble, if you catch my drift. So, you need your bestie to keep you out of trouble."

I scrunched up my face. "I hate it that you're right."

Zoe stood and walked over to me, throwing her arms around my neck. "Everything's going to be fine from here on out. We're here for two days. Let's make the most of it and forget what happened with Simmer."

"You're the best." I hugged Zoe back.

"Yes, I am. Now, go change and we'll head down to dinner and sign up for events. I'd love to go horseback riding tomorrow afternoon, so let's sign up before there are no more spots left."

I grabbed some clothing from my suitcase along with my toiletry bag and headed to the bathroom. After the miserable half hour I'd just lived through, I wanted more than a change of clothes to boost my confidence.

A thicker than normal layer of makeup applied to my eyes on top of a cute outfit later, I left the bathroom to hear a whistle from Zoe.

"Girl," Zoe shook her head and laughed. "Even if Simmering Simmons sees you again, he'll probably not recognize you as the girl who nearly took him out twice."

"Is that supposed to be flattering?" I cocked an eyebrow at her.

Still, she wasn't wrong. My long, wavy blonde hair shone after a good brushing and my high cheekbones did their job, along with the makeup, at bringing attention to my bright blue eyes. I'd even been lucky enough to inherit Dad's long eyelashes. They hadn't been layered in mascara earlier, so Bryce probably hadn't noticed them.

"He probably has a girlfriend." The thought both relieved and depressed me.

"Doesn't mean he can't look." Zoe winked at me.

I rolled my eyes. Zoe's notion remained that if there wasn't a ring on the finger, other fish in the pool were still eligible. Commitment and I didn't have a problem with each other. My last two boyfriends and I had been together for over two years each. They'd been the ones with the commitment issues.

"You make me feel like I need to gussy up along with you, but I'm starving, so let's go." Zoe grabbed her room key, a real key, not a digital card, and handed me my own. "When was the last time you were at a hotel and had a real key?"

We'd had the same discussion last year, but the key still amazed me. I'd expected to come back to updates like the key since last October. At this point, I didn't expect changes next year. But hey, if it worked for the Ranch, why change?

We left our room on the third floor, manually locking it behind us, and walked around the balcony which looked down onto the large lobby.

"I can't stand Halloween." Zoe shivered. "All the decorations creep me out."

I held my fist out and she bumped it with hers. Zoe and I had bonded over our lack of love for the holiday at hand. We spent Halloween night curled up on one of our couches watching Christmas movies. That was the holiday we could both get behind. Who couldn't love tinsel and presents?

We made it around the balcony to the open stairs before I

caught sight of Bryce and his buddies walking up toward us. The stairs had wooden railings like the rest of the balconies, and you could see the lobby and all the floors of the lodge if you stood on the landing between each of the three levels. The men were on their way up the second flight of stairs between levels two and three by the time Zoe noticed them.

She stiffened beside me and we both picked up speed to be past the men before Bryce noticed me. I even tilted my head to the side and down so my hair would shield my face from view. Why did I have to keep running into him? Quite literally. Well, this time I wouldn't.

Almost as soon as the thought crossed my mind, the heel of my shoe caught on a stair. The accident was enough to pitch me forward. Right into the path of the oncoming Bryce Simmons.

My boss' boss didn't even have time to look my way as I fell while he laughed with one of his friends. My body hitting his and toppling us both was his only warning before we rolled down the last few stairs to the landing.

"Oh ouch." Bryce winced as he pushed himself up from where he had landed on me. "Are you o-"

His question stopped as his brain recognized the woman who'd taken him out...again.

"Sorry?" I cringed.

Even the makeup wouldn't help me as he closed his eyes and shook his head, amusement making one side of his lips tilt up this time around. "Eloise?"

"Bryce, man, you okay?" One of Bryce's friends reached down and helped the overly attractive man to his feet.

I missed him on top of me already. That was a bad thought, but not only were his looks the desire of my girly parts, but he smelled so good. I'd have to do what I could to remember the smell because I'd never be that close to Bryce Simmons ever again. If this kept happening, I'd probably have a restraining order against me by the end of the weekend. Or I'd be fired. Or in a hospital as my poor body ached a bit too.

Zoe tried to help me to my feet, but a larger hand reached down for me. I couldn't meet Bryce's eyes as I accepted his help. Even when I stood, I bounced on the balls of my feet, waiting for a reprimand. He'd been far less than happy at our last encounter. Why was he amused this go around? Or was that fake?

Bryce crossed his arms over a broad chest and examined me. My heels gave me a couple inches extra height so Bryce and I looked each other straight in the eyes while we stood on the landing.

"Ms. Brandt, funny seeing you again." Bryce didn't appear hurt or in any sort of pain as he and his friends snickered. He'd obviously related our earlier encounters to them. Oh the joy.

The impression I received from Zoe behind me was that she'd like to run for the hills. She wasn't the only one.

"Mr. Simmons, no offense, but I was really hoping not to see you again on this trip. Honestly, I think the person to blame here is you."

Zoe groaned and I heard a hand slap a forehead as my bestie wanted to die. We'd known each other long enough for me to tell the signs.

On the other hand, Bryce's friends sputtered out laughter while Bryce's eyebrows rose in amused shock.

"Me?" He sputtered out when the shock could allow him to speak again. "How am I to blame?"

I gave an indifferent sort of shrug. "Well, I seem to have less accidents outside of when you're around. I haven't harmed Zoe," I threw a thumb over my shoulder to indicate my bestie, "in the year and a half we've known each other. Plus, I didn't pretty much tackle one of your friends because a heel caught on a stair. So, the obvious link in our encounters is you."

By the time I'd finished, one of Bryce's buddies, a burly man with a buzz cut laughed so hard he collapsed onto the stairs and tears poured down his eyes. Bryce rolled his eyes at him while sending a toe-curling smirk my way.

"Laugh it up, Bruce."

I blinked. The stocky man wasn't a friend, but Bryce's older brother. He oversaw a different division of the company.

"We'd best be going." Zoe wrapped her hand around my arm and tugged me toward the descending stairs.

"Let's not meet again this weekend?" Bryce laughed as Zoe and I raced down the stairs amid the laughter from the half dozen men.

"You really have some bad luck today, El." Zoe shook her head as we walked to the dining room.

"I need to go to bed early and wake up to a different day where my luck has changed." I winced as we walked. The pain in my ankle requested I do as I'd said, but Zoe already shook her head.

"No can do, lady. There's a magic act tonight, and we are not missing it."

Dinner was delicious and blessedly uneventful. We sat with Sally Rogers and her husband, Craig. They were newly-weds and Zoe and I both wanted to gag at the love shining in their eyes when they held hands and finished each other's sentences and laughed when they did.

"You're sure I can't sneak away?" I pouted as we sat near the front of the room where the magic show would take place. Another coworker, Allen, who had a massive crush on Zo, sat beside us. It was too bad she didn't feel the same way about him. He wasn't bad looking, but he wasn't Simmering Simmons either.

"You're not going anywhere." Zoe turned to me so Allen couldn't see her face and gave me pleading eyes. "You promised."

I'd done no such thing, but besties saved their bestie. Like it or not, I'd be sitting through a magic show.

When Bryce and his gang walked in the door to our left, I shrunk in my chair. Thankfully for my sanity, they didn't see me and walked toward the other side of the room. And nothing outside of the norm happened. Zoe and I both let out breaths I didn't know we'd held after the men passed us by.

"Scared of the boss?" Allen laughed at us.

"Let's just say it's been a day for Eloise." Zoe wrapped an arm around my shoulders and squeezed as a man made his way onto the stage.

The magician didn't even have to call the room to order as we quieted and waited on him to speak.

"Welcome, welcome! You're all looking quite excited tonight. Men, did you dine with your wives? Ladies, did he give you roses?"

With sleight of hand I couldn't figure out, the magician with his handlebar mustache, dark hair, and gleaming eyes created a dozen roses out of thin air. The crowd clapped. Some whistled. I squinted to figure out the play.

"Don't figure it out, Eloise." Zoe jabbed me in the ribs. "It takes away the fun."

"Maybe for some."

"You're no fun to take to these events."

I opened my mouth to say I'd requested to leave, but closed it when Zo glared my way, a reminder why I'd stayed. She should relax. Allen wasn't going to jump her with so many people around. He was one of the nicest guys in the office and wouldn't be jumping her at all.

The magician went through trick after trick. None of them I could figure out. Squinting harder didn't help.

"Now, it's the time everyone has been waiting for. I need two volunteers." The magician looked around at the crowd of volunteers waving their hands. "You, there. Yes, you."

I'd pointed to myself, sure I was mistaken about him asking me to join him on the stage. After all, my hand hadn't been raised.

"Go, El." Zoe pushed me, and I climbed from my chair.

"And you, sir," the magician called to another volunteer, who may or may not have been volunteering, to come join me on the stage.

I fought a groan when Bryce climbed up the stairs on the other side of the stage. He could only shake his head and smile.

"Do the two of you know each other?" The magician had caught our reaction and my face ignited. The people in the very back could probably see me glow without a problem.

"We just met tonight." Bryce saved me so much embarrassment by keeping his answer vague and succinct. Or, he was saving himself the humiliation. Either way, I came out of the situation in better shape than I'd feared.

The magician waggled his eyebrows. "Must have been some sort of meeting with the way she's blushing, young man."

Bryce shrugged. The magician looked to me and I gave the same reaction. The crowd laughed when the magician turned to them and gave the same answer.

"Alright, here comes the fun part. I'll ask you to stand beside each other." He pushed us so our arms touched. "It's not required, but I thought it'd be fun."

He winked at the crowd, who laughed. Meanwhile, I wanted to dig a hole as Zoe also blushed and shook her head. I couldn't look at Bryce. Simmering Simmons was way over his head today if he thought our track record had ceased. My gut told me we were in for a lot of trouble.

3

The magician stood in front of Bryce and spoke so the crowd could hear him. "Stare at this coin. When I snap my fingers, you'll go to sleep."

Bryce rubbed his hands together in excitement. If only I could follow his lead. Instead, apprehension flooded me. I prayed the magician didn't make me do anything stupid in front of all my coworkers, their families, and people from other offices. I'd already embarrassed myself enough privately for one day. I didn't need to do the same in the public view. Plus, this event hadn't even been on my list of things to do during our vacation. Zoe owed me.

The magician's snap brought me back to the present. Bryce's head slumped forward, and the magician patted his shoulder while the crowd clapped. During the noise of their laughter and applause, words slipped from the magician's mouth. I couldn't understand the words but they sounded like Latin I'd heard in school. The vibes coming from them sent a chill up my spine and I shivered.

The magician spoke for a short time, not long enough for the crowd to notice or think him weird, and pulled back. I kept my eyes diverted from him and gave the crowd a small smile.

"Now, with another snap of my finger, we'll put this young lady to sleep. Then, the real fun starts." The magician laughed along with the crowd and my stomach twisted. Were his words in Bryce's ear part of the act? They'd sounded more sinister than fun, but he'd whispered them so maybe they were a part the crowd didn't need to hear? Was that how the act worked?

The magician walked me through the same steps as Bryce.

I blinked and the crowd applauded. When had they started clapping so hard?

I blinked, disoriented. Zoe laughed and smiled in her seat as she and Allen clapped with the crowd. Seeing my bestie unworried calmed my unease. If something bad had happened, she wouldn't be laughing.

Bryce moved beside me. He gave a small wave and a smile to the crowd, but up close, I could see the small tension lines on his face and the fact his smile was forced. The man even looked a bit ill but pushed the feeling aside to give a good show to those he oversaw. He didn't want to appear weak.

The magician closed the show out fast after that and I didn't have a moment to nab the scoop from Zoe before the crowd clapped for a final time and everyone stood to disperse.

"That was such a fun show!" Zoe beamed as we left the large room behind. People smiled at me as we left which continued to eat at me. What had I done while hypnotized?

"I think I'm headed to bed now." My body's exhaustion

had doubled since dinner even if my mind was fully awake. Was that the fault of the magician and his act?

Zoe pouted until she noticed Allen had left with us and stood just behind her elbow. "I think you're probably right. With the day you've had, someone needs to make sure you arrive at the room safely."

"I could help escort her?" Allen was so sweet with his hesitant request that came out more as a question of allowing him rather than offer.

"I have this, but thank you."

"No problem."

Zoe grabbed my elbow and tugged, but it wasn't my day. My body used the momentum to keep spinning and fall over. Well, I began to fall over.

"Hang on there." The all too familiar voice made me groan as Bryce helped me stand upright. "You are having an awful day, aren't you, Eloise?"

"Could be better."

"Since you're bound to bump into me and kill me sometime tonight, why don't I just walk you to your room so there's no opportunity for you to take us both out?"

"It's okay. Zoe was about to take me." When I glanced at my bestie, she nodded, and her wide eyes begged me to high-tail it out of there with her.

"Why doesn't Zoe take the night off of best friend duty? I can keep you safe for five minutes. Besides, there's something I'd like to discuss with you."

Allen cleared his throat before more than the idea of losing my job crossed my mind. I was toast.

"I could buy Ms. Dean a drink or something."

Bryce pulled a bill from his wallet and handed it to Allen while Zoe glared at me. I'd already found myself in trouble. There was no way on this earth I wanted to make that worse for myself. I'd have her back the next time she needed it. For now, having a drink with Allen wouldn't be the end of her world. Unlike mine.

"Right this way, Zoe." Allen gave a small bow in the direction of the lodge's restaurant and Zoe glared at me one more time for good measure.

"Apologize for me later?" Bryce didn't look at all apologetic. "They just look good together, and I really do want to talk with you."

They did look good, but Zoe could look good with the oldest, ugliest man on Earth. She was beautiful.

"Are you alright?" Bryce took my elbow like Zoe had tried to do and had failed. The man's friends were by the stairs. They gave Bryce a thumbs up and I glanced to the floor as he waved them off. "Come on, this way before they act like goons."

He led me through the thinning crowd, most of whom appeared intrigued by us together. They could be intrigued all they wanted because this was only me getting fired. I'd be leaving tomorrow on the hunt for another job.

Bryce gave a heavy exhale when we exited the lodge's front doors.

"That was pretty intense back there." I nodded my head back toward the lodge. "I wasn't expecting to be called on. My hand wasn't in the air. Zoe dragged me to the show, or I would be catching some Z's right now. I also wouldn't have nearly killed you again."

We walked down the stairs, past the cars, to the other side

of the parking lot. A brisk wind blew through my sweater and I shivered.

"Are you cold?" Bryce watched me with concern, but I waved him off.

"If we're not out here too long, I'll be okay."

Disappointment made him frown. "I'd actually thought you and I might take a little walk. Go to the stables and see the horses or something."

I blinked at him. "Really?"

"Yeah, why else would I bring you out here?"

I bit my lips together. No way could I tell him my thoughts, but his smile was disarming and I blurted out the answer he wanted.

"I was pretty sure you were about to fire me."

"Fire you?" He took a step back, confused and appalled at the thought. "Why would I fire you?"

My turn came to blink at him. "Um, I did open my door into you, disturb you in the bathroom and fell on you when you opened the door, and then I did fall into you walking down the stairs enough that we took a tumble down them. Oh, that doesn't count me falling into you again after the show tonight."

His amusement shone in the light from the full moon. While dark, everything remained visible with such a bright light in the sky.

"I wouldn't fire you because of that. People have bad days. At first, yes, I was grumpy about it for which I'm sorry. Dad's been gruff and I can't get him to open up about what's bothering him. Bruce and I have both tried. I'd just been on the phone with him again and he was short with me, but the guys banded together to cheer me up and once in a better mood, I realized what a jerk I'd been. I'm very sorry for that."

"You weren't that bad." Another shiver went through me. "Maybe I'll go grab a jacket if you don't mind."

"Sure. Would you like me to walk you in?"

"No, it's alright. I'll be back in just a couple minutes."

I turned and walked back to the lodge, shaking my head. How could a guy like Bryce Simmons, a man so hot he was called Simmering, want to spend his time with me? I was a little nobody in the company. My job was menial paper pushing. Even if the company couldn't function without my job, they could most certainly function without me. People liked Bryce. They respected him. I was a clutz who'd had the worst day of all bad days. No, it wasn't my normal, but some people thought me too chatty.

Most of the lodge's occupants had cleared out by the time I reentered the lobby. My memory jogged and I couldn't help but smile at the cackling witch by the hallway which led to the bathrooms. Maybe my day wasn't turning out half bad after all. My embarrassment had led to time with Bryce.

Zoe was still out with Allen when I returned to the room. We'd only been gone five minutes, so I hadn't expected her back yet. Allen would do his best to keep her entertained and with him for as long as possible, I was sure. Maybe once she actually gave the man a chance, she'd find she liked him.

Since Bryce had said he'd drop me off, I left a note for Zoe in case she beat me back to the room. Then I grabbed up my fleece jacket and locked the door behind me.

I'd been asked on a walk with Bryce Simmons. Yes, it was just a walk, not a date, but he'd asked me. Me!

The lobby had emptied completely by the time I hit the

main floor again. My bladder gave a warning and I bit my lip. I hadn't been long, but would Bryce think I'd run off and wouldn't come back? However, I didn't want to excuse myself from our walk to use the bathroom. I'd already had enough embarrassing experiences because of a full bladder. I didn't need more.

No one occupied the bathroom down the short hallway this time around. My nerves relaxed when the door opened with ease. Part of me, or more, was now glad it had been occupied earlier.

The lobby remained empty when I left the bathroom. Even the front desk didn't have the staff manning it as usual. The phone rang, but no one raced to answer. A bad feeling settled into my gut. What was happening? Where was the staff?

Glass broke down the long hallway which led to the restaurant. A nervous curiosity led me in that direction, needing to find a reason why the hundred or so people in the lodge were oddly absent and quiet. I'd check the restaurant next and find Zoe.

"I'm sorry, Nick. I know you're upset, but let's talk this out like grown adults."

The deep, forced calm voice drew me to a stop beside a slightly open door on the left down the hallway. It was the same room the magic act had been held in. Who was still there?

"I'm tired of talking! Twenty-five years I've worked for you and you do this to me!" The short, stocky man I saw as I peeked into the room threw another glass against the wall and I jumped. The room had been changed over to allow tables to be set up instead of rows of chairs. There were a lot of glasses he could destroy.

"Nick, he graduated with his masters and has experience as a manager already." The man I recognized from pictures as Bryce's dad, Henry Simmons, the company president, held his hands up to placate the disgruntled man who had to be an employee. "I know you've been with us for a long time, and I've offered you a generous raise-"

"It's not good enough!" Nick's face was beet red and my heart raced as he took a few aggressive steps forward in the direction of Mr. Simmons.

"Calm down now, Nick, or you can consider yourself fired with advice to go see a counselor for anger management." Henry appeared unfazed by the angered man.

"No need to fire me, Simmons. I quit!"

"Fine." Mr. Simmons' face took on a stone-cold glint as his anger rose visibly for the first time during the conversation. "No need for a two weeks' notice."

"You'll regret this, Simmons." Nick laughed and the evil sound of a madman made the hair on the back of my neck rise. "I've given my life to your company and your family. Life I can't get back. But never mind that. I knew you wouldn't change your mind. That's why I hired that magician."

Mr. Simmons' face paled and my stomach plummeted.

"What are you talking about? What magician? Tonight's magician?"

Nick laughed harder. He'd turned from me so I could no longer see his face, but from the sound of his voice, he was quite pleased with himself.

"A life for a life, Simmons. You took twenty-five years of my life. Now I'm taking twenty-five years from you in the form of your son."

"Leave Bryce out of this!"

Nick held up a hand. "What's done is done. By morning, Bryce will have met the fate you caused for him."

Bryce. He was outside. Alone.

I turned as voices raised again and ran down the still empty hallway. The empty lobby didn't slow me down to think of the staff's absence. Bryce had a target on his back. For once today, I'd been in the right spot at the right time.

4

The brisk wind slapped me in the face as I rushed from the lodge. My mind whirled a thousand miles an hour and I missed the first step leading down to the parking lot. Thankfully, Bryce was there to catch me. Again.

"Whoa, Eloise, where's the fire?" He chuckled as he righted me. His smile fell when he took in my panic. "What is it?"

"We need to run. Go. Now."

I grabbed his hand and tried to pull him down the steps with me, but he wouldn't budge.

"Hold up. What's happening?" Bryce held my hand tighter and cupped my cheek to make me look at him.

Tears stung my eyes. Fear threatened to choke me and hold my feet in place, but I couldn't allow that. There was no time to give in to the fear, so until I could give in, I had to focus on one thing: making Bryce come with me.

"I know you don't know me, but please, please, I need you to trust me. Just for a few minutes. Please, let's go somewhere now."

Bryce wiped at my face. Moisture trailed his thumb. I was crying?

Another agonizing minute passed before Bryce nodded.

"Let's go take that walk and you can tell me what's going on."

This time, he allowed me to pull him down the stairs, but I didn't lead him to the barn as we'd planned. Instead, I led him toward the fields where we'd ride horses tomorrow. And we would. Bryce wouldn't die tonight.

Bryce kept pace with me as I rushed into a grassy field outside of the fenced in area where the horses grazed. Forests skirted the field and I pulled him in their direction. They'd provide the cover we needed.

"Hey, hey, hold up." Bryce pulled me so I spun back to look at him. Worry, and a tad bit of apprehension glinted back at me in the full moon's light. "What is going on?"

"Someone put a hit on your head."

He blinked. "Excuse me?"

I pulled my hand from his and began pacing a few feet in front of him as I spoke. My hands waved in the air as I relived the conversation I'd overheard. The movement kept my hands from shaking.

"A guy named Nick fought with your dad in the room where the magic act was tonight. There weren't fists. Just words. I didn't look in on them to spy. I heard glass break when I left the bathroom and then the yelling so I checked it out on the sly.

"When I did, your dad and that Nick guy fought about something, someone, and Nick wasn't happy. Said your dad took twenty-five years of his life and now he was going to take twenty-five years from your dad in the form of your life."

I shook and when I finished my explanation, the world

tilted. My body pitched to the side, forcing Bryce to again correct me so I didn't fall.

"Nick Delaney, was it him?"

My hands gripped Bryce's biceps in a tight hold to steady myself, grounding my emotions. "I don't know. All I know was his name was Nick and he was upset about some guy with a master's degree and manager experience."

Bryce groaned. "Yeah, it's Nick Delaney. He missed out on a promotion a month or so ago. I didn't realize he was sore enough about it to make threats."

"This is more than a threat, Bryce. He already has a plan in play, or that's what he told your dad. Nick said something about the magician and you dying tonight, or at least you being dead by morning. We have to keep you away from the lodge until then." I grabbed at his hand, but Bryce evaded me.

"What about Dad and Bruce?"

"Nick wants twenty-five years, Bryce. That's what's important to him. How old is Bruce?"

My eyes continued to scan the moonlit darkness while we talked. The magician had creeped me out with his Latin sounding words. I wasn't a believer in magic or anything like that–I'd tried to discover the magician's tricks after all–but something about the Latin had made me nervous. So nervous I'd almost run off the stage if I'd had time.

"Bruce is twenty-seven. How old are you, Eloise?"

"Twenty-three, but that's irrelevant. I'm not the one with a hit on my head by a crazy man, and trust me, Bryce, he might not have been crazy before, but he's batty now. And I know I sound crazy myself, but I swear I'm not. Even if I've had a bad day. I heard this and I was in my right mind." My voice cracked as my eyes burned again. Would he ever believe me?

Bryce opened his mouth and closed it again with a heavy exhale. He didn't believe me, but I couldn't give up. How could I convince him?

His phone buzzed before Bryce could think of something to say to me. I wrapped my arms around myself as the chilly autumn wind drove a cloud in front of the moon, diminishing almost all the light we had to see by.

"Hello? Hey, Dad. No, I'm not in the lodge. Wait, slow down." Bryce's body began to stiffen as his father continued to speak.

A horse whinnied nearby. We were on a ranch with horses, but the noise sounded more ominous than normal, and closer, but I was hyped up more than normal. Still, I looked around. From the field where we stood, the noise could sound like it came from anywhere.

"Okay, Dad, I'll keep an eye about me. No, I'm not telling you where I am in case that's his ploy. Go find Bruce and stay with him in case I'm a distraction and Nick wants to hurt him. Breathe and we'll figure this out. Also, get some sleep. You sound beyond exhausted."

The cloud moved off the moon as Bryce continued to talk and the horse noises grew closer. I turned in a slow circle, watching the darkened forest around the field. When the cloud fully moved and Bryce ended his conversation, I stilled, frozen with more fear than I'd ever known.

"Okay, let's find somewhere safe-" Bryce stopped talking when I hit him. "What is it?"

My finger shook as I pointed toward the tree line closer to the lodge. Bryce gasped as he took in the man on top of the large steed. The horse wasn't so much breathtaking–though the black horse's huge size made me gulp along with the fact puffs of mist escaped his mouth every time he breathed and his eyes glowed red–as the man was. The man with no head.

Bryce came out of his shock first, which was good because my body had no plans of doing so until Bryce crouched a little in front of me and held a finger to his lips to quiet me. Then he motioned to another section of forest, the section closest to us that also jutted out into the field.

We didn't speak as we carefully made our way to the trees. Fear still ate at me so bad my eyes blurred and burned with tears, but I didn't sniffle even when I wanted to. Even when the tears spilled over down my cheeks, blinding me, I kept my feet moving, guided by Bryce who held himself together better than I did. Until a twig snapped beneath my feet, echoing in the darkness.

Bryce and I both gasped as we turned to the figure, still headless, on his horse. The horse whinnied again at the sound and its rider turned in the saddle to look our way. Even without a head, it was as if eyes could see us and a coy smile rose when we were spotted.

"Run." Bryce pushed me forward toward the trees as the horse took off in our direction. Mist poured from its mouth in the cool air.

When I didn't move fast enough, Bryce leapt forward, pulling me after him. The trees engulfed us and the light from the moon diminished. Even with the loss of leaves, the forest was so thick and filled with pines whose branches started halfway up the tree that the moon's light was mostly blocked completely, making running difficult. At least for me.

"Come on, Eloise!" Bryce kept a tight hold of my hand and I focused more on him than my surroundings. If I didn't keep up, I'd trip and take us both down. The neighing horse behind us, and its rider, would love that.

"Guess I was right," I puffed as we ran.

"I'd say so, but I'd like to know who that guy is." Bryce didn't sound winded at all. After this, I'd be hitting the gym. The treadmill would be my new best friend.

"He's the headless horseman! Surely you know the tale!"

"Yeah, but this isn't Sleepy Hollow, El. We're nowhere near New York. Besides, ouch, Dad said the magician's in on it, so it's probably a ploy we have to figure out."

"He spoke…in…Latin when…he…hypno…tized…you." The more we ran, the less I could talk between deep breaths.

"Did he speak in Latin when he hypnotized you?"

"I can't…remember…anything. I…only know…he spoke…to you…because…I wasn't…asleep yet."

"Breathe and run, El. You can do this." Bryce tightened his hand around mine and pushed tree limbs away from me as best he could, but my face and body were still assaulted by them as we continued plunging into the forest. One of us was bound to lose an eye and with the way my luck went today, it'd be me.

Sweat rolled down my back by the time Bryce stopped us. "I don't hear them."

I couldn't hear anything over my heavy breathing and racing heart. I'd have to trust the man who was barely winded. Around us, the forest remained empty and dark. A shudder passed through me and I wasn't ashamed to press myself against Bryce's front and hold onto his shirt. He was kind enough to wrap his arms around me, giving me the comfort I needed.

"We'll be okay, El. We probably overreacted."

He sounded as convinced as I was, and I wasn't convinced at all.

Bryce gave a heavy sigh. "We need to find that magician. He knows what's going on."

I looked up at him. "What'll we do if Headless is still out there?"

Bryce pulled me closer with his arms. His hands rubbed up and down my back as I trembled against him.

"We'll be okay. Nick said I had until sunrise, right?" I nodded against his shoulder. "Well, then I just stay alive until sunrise. Even if we have to stay out here all night. I need to get you back to the lodge though where you'll be safe."

I'd begun to shake my head and he glared down at me in the little light we had.

"I'm not going anywhere, Bryce. I may be accident prone today, but I'm not all the time. Most days I'm coordinated. I know that's a bit unbelievable right now, but it's the truth. My luck isn't really as bad as it seems today."

A roll of thunder passed over us, followed by the sky opening the floodgates. We were soaked in seconds.

"You were saying?" Bryce laughed as I groaned and buried my face into his shoulder. His hands couldn't rub my back as easily with my wet clothes, but he didn't stop holding me.

Another whinny behind Bryce stilled us. I looked up at Simmering Simmons, but couldn't see him through the rain I had to squint my eyes against.

"Let's go. They're close but not on top of us." Bryce pulled me behind him.

I did my best to stay quiet, but I could no longer see and stumbled over branches and other debris on the ground. Bryce had to catch me every time I tripped. The darkness and the storm blinded me to everything. If Bryce weren't with me, I wouldn't have made it nearly as far as we did together.

There was enough time for Bryce to yell, "Watch out!", but not enough time for me to react, when pain exploded in my face with a loud crack. I went down. So much for my luck improving at all.

5

Water drops hit me in the face. Someone called my name. Pain screamed at the bridge of my nose and across my right cheek.

"Eloise! El, can you hear me?" He cradled my head in his hands, turning my face side to side.

"Bryce?"

I used my tongue to gauge if I'd lost any teeth as my brain began to function further.

"Eloise! Thank goodness! Can you stand?" Bryce pulled me to sit up. "Your nose is bleeding, but we need to run, El. They're close."

They, who were they?

A horse gave a high-pitched whinny and the vision of a black horse pawing at the ground with its headless rider staring at Bryce and I took my breath away.

"Help me," I begged while trying to push myself to my feet. My coordination still didn't work right, but with Bryce's help I found my feet. I just couldn't stay on them and sank back to the ground to sit in the mud.

"I'm so sorry. I didn't realize the branch would snap back like that." Bryce held my head still but, in the darkness, I couldn't make his face out. Not to mention, the rain continued to cascade down. "I need to find help for you. At least I need to return you to the lodge."

"He's after you, Bryce. If he gets too close to us, run. He'll ignore me."

"I'm not leaving you."

"Again, he's not after me. He's after you. Wait." I pulled my keys from my pants pocket. "Go to my car. In the trunk, there's a sword."

"A sword?"

"My dad's. I'm not sure if this thing can die from a sword, but we can try if things become that bleak."

Bryce pushed my keys away. "If things become that dire, you'll be safely locked in your room which is where I'm taking you."

"No! He'll catch us. You need to hide, Bryce. Find some-where safe to stay until the sun comes up. I'll go back to the lodge and find some help."

"Go back to the lodge? El, you can't even hold your head up." He just had to bring up my weakness, didn't he? I tried to prove him wrong, but my head wouldn't stay up. "Give your-self another minute."

"You need to go, Bryce."

"How long have you worked at the company?"

I blinked at Bryce through the rain. "Why are you changing the subject?"

He snorted into the darkness. "I'm about to die by the hands of a fictional being on his fog breathing horse. Part of me is about to be sent into a full-blown panic. You, along with my need to care for you, are the only things keeping me sane.

So, humor me for a moment please. This might be my last night on Earth and I'd like to spend it how I wish."

"And how's that?"

"With you. So far, you're the most entertaining woman I've ever met. Again, I'm sorry for the way I acted when we first met."

"It's all good. I probably could have acted a bit better the second time we met, but I seriously had to use the bathroom. It's been nothing but bad luck ever since."

Bryce laughed quietly. A man with no head couldn't hear us, could he? He'd managed to see us, though, hadn't he?

"You were fine, El. I'm really glad to have met you. If nothing else, you've made my last few hours of life quite entertaining. Can you stand?" He helped me to my feet again and held me until the world stopped spinning.

"I've worked at the company for two years. I'm not important to the overall company. My job is in the front office in an outbuilding, but the job was there when I needed it out of college. Now, I stay because Zoe works there too, and I don't live far from my parents."

"How long have you known Zoe?"

He took my hand and we began moving away from the sounds of the horse. This time, there would be no stick cracking beneath my foot to give us away. The rain was too loud for that. Still, I kept my voice down when I spoke to him, forcing Bryce to lean down to hear me.

"She was hired six months after me. Just when I'd decided to try finding another job. We hit it off instantly and she's like the sister I've never had. Zo's in marketing, though. She has a brilliant mind. One day, if I live long enough, since I'm now accident prone, I want to be like her."

"What's your favorite animal?"

"Well, it's certainly not horses." We chuckled, but they were both forced laughter. Bryce really was as nervous as he admitted to being and my face was killing me. "What did you want to talk about on our walk tonight?"

The horse whinnied, closer this time. Bryce led me faster through the forest by his side, away from the noise, and kept a vigilant effort to protect my sore face.

"Do you even know where we are?" My voice trembled as the rain died down to a sprinkle and the sound of a horse galloping came closer.

"Not really, but I need you to run, El."

Bryce pulled me forward quicker as my heart began to beat hard again. Breathing became more difficult through a swollen nose which might have been broken. I still couldn't see where to put my foot and if luck held out, bad luck that is, I'd be breaking an ankle sometime soon.

When we hit flat land and no trees, I sighed internally in relief. The new terrain would make running easier.

"We need to get off this trail." Bryce pulled me into the next set of forest as galloping hooves sounded behind us.

I shrieked and ducked with Bryce in time for an ax to chop down a sapling beside us where our heads had been.

"Run!" Bryce pulled me along behind him again as I looked over my shoulder. Rider and horse were turning around for another pass. The moon peeked out from behind a cloud enough to give me another look at the headless form.

I screamed at the ghastly sight of the rider raising his large ax to swing at us again. His clothes were old style and the horse's eyes still glowed red like a demon. Then, Bryce had us in the forest running for our lives. This time, wood split as the pair attempted to follow us.

"Bryce, you have to go!" I pulled my hand from his grip.

"I'm not leaving you behind." He looked back at the noise behind us.

I wanted to rescind my offer for him to go, but I'd already slowed him down. "I'll be fine. Run."

"I can't."

Wood splintered closer to us. I whimpered. "Go, Bryce, before he reaches us. He's not after me. Go. Here, have my keys."

Bryce's warm lips crashed onto my forehead as he took my keys from my hand. "Be safe, Eloise, or I'll never forgive myself."

Bryce dashed off in the next second. Where was he headed? To my car or deeper into the forest? The darkness threatened to suffocate me as I sat on the ground and curled in on myself, wrapping my arms around raised knees. Did Bryce even know which way led back to the lodge and my car?

Horse hooves galloping away nearly made me shriek until they faded into the distance. Bryce hadn't taken the trail with Headless so close. The trees would slow Bryce down, but they'd also slow down the horse and his rider. As long as Bryce and I stayed where the forest's trees were thick, we could survive this, right? But there was so much open land around the lodge and stables. Would Headless catch up to Bryce then?

I rose to my feet. Pain made me nauseous along with the taste of blood in my mouth, but I could do this. I could help Bryce. Determination helped me step forward. I'd have to hurry to delay Headless. Somehow. Both he and Bryce had a head start on me, but Bryce could hide if I slowed the horse.

Ignoring the way Bryce had gone, I went to the trail the horses followed during the rides we could sign up for while here, the trail the demon horse had ridden on. I'd been scheduled to ride tomorrow if I still lived. However, I decided to pass and spend the day inside sleeping. How many hours until sunrise?

I pulled my phone from my back pocket while hobbling as fast as I could down the trail. I'd never beat the horse wherever it went, but I'd give it my best to meet up with it. My luck remained the same. The phone was as dead as a doornail.

The further I walked, the more my shoes began to sink into the new mud of the path. They made a squishing noise when I pulled them up, so I tried to walk closer to the trees and side of the path using my hands out in front of me to keep me from walking into a tree. Any chance I'd had to see hoofprints had been washed away by the rain and hidden by the clouds over the moon.

When I believed I'd remain in the forest forever, the trees opened up to the field. My shoulders fell. We'd run much further from the lodge than I'd expected. In a brief sliver of moonlight, I couldn't see either Bryce or Headless. Had Bryce arrived at my car safely or had he been overtaken by the headless man on his mount?

I shivered as I took a step forward into the field.

"Just put one foot in front of the other, Eloise. Just keep walking. Find Bryce or…" Or find Headless, but I couldn't say that out loud. Deep down, or very shallow down, I didn't want to find Headless. I wanted him to go away with the sunrise, but Bryce and I had gone to take our walk at least an hour before midnight. Time in the dark was hard to tell, but we weren't at sunrise yet. There was still too much time before sun made its appearance in the sky. Even a minute was too long.

Somehow, foot after foot, I made my way to the stable. Horses made some noise inside, but no humans were about. From a corner of the barn, I couldn't make out any people around the lodge either. The front lights on the building shone down into the parking lot, but I couldn't tell if my car had been intentionally tampered with by Bryce.

I ran from the barn closest to the lodge to the side of the lodge itself and peeked my head around the corner. Bryce's SUV blocked my car from view. Had he made it to my trunk?

"Walk to the car. Check the trunk. Find Bryce." I repeated the instructions aloud a few times before I found the nerve to follow through. The darkness didn't help. Neither did the silence that seemed to want to crush me. The lodge's occupants were actually sleeping through the worst night of my life.

I stepped around the corner of the building. My feet crunched on gravel and my heart stopped, but nothing else stirred around me. Another step and still nothing. No birds. No crickets. No owls even. Could they sense the predator running amok tonight?

When I reached Bryce's car, my body trembled so bad I had to hug my stomach to keep my arms and hands from hitting anything. Memories flooded my mind as I walked between his SUV and my small car. Had only hours passed since I hit him with my car door?

At the back of the car, the trunk remained closed. Without

my key to open the lid, that told me nothing. Bryce could have come and gone and closed the trunk behind him. Or, he might not have made it to the car yet. Headless was after him, not me, so my journey back to the lodge was probably a lot easier than Bryce's.

I leaned my elbows onto my trunk, facing the lodge, and held the sides of my face with my hands. With the rain, I couldn't tell if my nose still bled. It still hurt. Was Bryce hurt? Maybe I should have stayed with him.

A horse whinnied and I spun to find myself looking into a black horse's red gaze. He breathed out and mist smacked me in the face. The chill of it froze me to the bones.

"Look out!"

Someone grabbed me from behind and hauled me out of the way as Headless' ax came down on the back of my car, splitting the trunk in two.

6

"Come on!" The magician pulled me along toward the building. What was he doing here?

Horse hooves clopped behind us as we burst into the lobby of the lodge. The lights blazed, but everyone remained missing. Tears filled my eyes as I blinked against the pain of the light against my eyes which were used to the darkness outside.

"This way!" The magician led me down the hallway on our left toward the restaurant and room where we'd had the magic show. Unlike Bryce, this man didn't care how he handled me. I'd be bruised after this.

The magician swung open the door to the room where Bryce's dad and Nick argued, also the room where the magician had hypnotized Bryce and I. This room had bad memories all around and I wanted nothing to do with it, but once inside, the magician flipped off the lights and pressed his body against mine. He didn't seem to care that he crushed me between himself and the wall.

"Quiet." The magician's breaths came in fast gasps and he glistened with sweat.

"What is going on?" I kept my voice down but the man hissed at me.

"Do you want to die? Then be quiet!"

"What is going on?" This time I spoke a little louder. He could at least answer that one question so I could leave and find Bryce.

"Shut up! We're all supposed to be asleep right now. The creature is supposed to kill anything that moves."

That meant…

"He's not after Bryce?"

"He is, but you're supposed to be asleep and I'm supposed to be out of here. That guy who hired me, Nick something, he slashed my tires. Now, shut up!"

Footsteps down the hallway caused the man to whimper. Well, I'd found out answers, but it looked like I wouldn't live long enough to tell them to anyone. Headless was after my head too which meant leaving the forest had been a bad idea.

Why wasn't I asleep? He'd hypnotized me too. Was that where everyone was? Sleeping? If the magician could create Headless, I didn't doubt he could put everyone to sleep. And here I hadn't believed in magic.

Wood splintered beside us as the door flew across the room. I screamed. The magician drug me after him deeper into the room and away from the door, keeping me between himself and Headless. The ax in Headless' hand was raised, ready to take off my head. It was so big, the blade probably could take both my head and the magician's off in the same swipe.

My heart pounded and if the magician hadn't kept backing us up around the now set up tables away from his monster, then I'd have been glued to the floor. Thankfully

I'd used the bathroom earlier or I would have also wet my pants.

"Go away! Go kill the boy! He's your target!" The magician's voice broke as terror consumed him.

"What was the Latin for on the stage?" That was the last question I wanted answered before the night was through. Well, more like before the night was through for me and I died.

"The spell would keep Bryce Simmons awake tonight. He won't tire. Not until he's dead or the sun rises."

"Why the sunrise?"

"Because that's how much the guy paid me for. He couldn't afford until the boy was dead or for an exact target. Now I realize I should have done that anyway."

The magician threw me forward into Headless' path, but for once, my bad luck wasn't so bad. I tripped over chairs and somehow, painfully, ended up beneath a table.

"No! No!"

A thud proceeded the magician's head rolling beneath my table. I held a hand over my mouth to keep from screaming. Light from the hallway filtered into the room enough for me to see the man's open eyes and blood pooling at the base of his severed neck. He'd done this to us, but had he deserved to die?

I did shriek when the ax sliced through the table inches from my toes. The half table and chairs made it hard to scramble out of the mess and when I did, I barely ducked in time to keep my head attached to my body.

My eyes were as big as saucers as Headless raised his ax once more. This time, I wouldn't be lucky enough to duck. My one bit of good luck for the night was gone. My breaths came too fast. If I were lucky, I'd pass out before he decapitated me.

Someone roared. I flinched, but it wasn't the creature. Someone behind the monster drove a sword through the monster's middle. Headless didn't flinch but turned to expose Bryce to me.

"Run, El!"

My feet listened as my brain fumbled, but I ran from the room without trouble, Bryce right behind me.

"The sword was a good idea," Bryce grasped at my hand as we fled the building, the headless man behind us, "but I'm afraid it didn't work."

"Now where?" I swung my head back and forth. Complete darkness met my sight. The light from inside had ruined my night vision.

"Trees. Let's go."

Bryce ran, my hand in his, through the parking lot toward the nearest part of the forest. We came to an abrupt halt as a horse appeared and reared up on its hind legs in front of us.

"This way!" Bryce pulled me back toward the building. Headless was on his way down the stairs. "Climb in!"

Climb in?

The lights on his car blinked. Oh, climb in! If we could make it in time before Headless reached us we'd be good to go.

I opened the door and climbed into the vehicle. Bryce yelled a warning as Headless' ax took off my door. The engine started and Bryce wasted no time reversing out of his space. Tires kicked up dirt as he shifted gears and we raced away from Headless down the driveway to the road. Bryce didn't stop when we reached the pavement but turned right, the way I'd arrived at the Ranch.

"Buckle up, El."

Had my brain not been overrun with terror, I'd have thought of that once the car was in motion being that I had no door keeping me in the vehicle. I did as Bryce said and closed my eyes. My body was still hyped up, but we were on the road. We were racing away from the danger. When daylight came, we could go back to the Ranch.

"Of all the bad luck in the world!" Bryce hit the steering wheel as he glared into the rearview mirror. "They're following us."

"They're what? How?"

"Demon horses can go as fast as they want, apparently." Bryce gripped the wheel tighter. "Hold on. I'll see if we can go faster to beat them, but don't hold your breath."

I gripped my seat belt, too afraid now to close my eyes. If death was coming for me in the form of a car accident, I didn't know if it was better to see it coming or face it without knowledge. Seeing as how my eyes refused to leave the road, I'd say I picked seeing my demise.

"Hold on. They're coming up on your side." Bryce moved the car to the left lane, and I could see us hitting someone head on. What way was better to die? Loss of head or head on collision? I was still young. I tried not to think too often about how I would die. Living was my preferred option.

Movement outside my door caught my attention. Demon red eyes looked over at me from the horse's head. Its rider leaned forward, ax in hand, motivating the horse in silence to run faster. How could the monster even see to know where he was going?

"Down!"

Metal shrieked and the car wobbled and skittered on the road as Headless' ax tore through the frame above my head, shattering part of the windshield and spiderwebbing the rest. Bryce's side of the SUV remained intact, but my side was being opened like a can of tuna fish. How long could the vehicle last? We'd been lucky not to swerve off the road, but my luck wasn't on its best behavior tonight.

"Brace yourself!"

"Now what?" I couldn't handle more. My stomach wanted to vomit.

Bryce braked. Hard. My body pushed against the seatbelt and I reached for the dash to help the belt in case it faltered on its job. And I screamed. Tears blurred my vision. If fear didn't kill me, Headless would.

The car fishtailed as we slowed, but Bryce kept us from dying. He didn't let us come to a full stop before we pulled a U-turn in the road and sped back to the Ranch.

"We're going to die. We're going to die. We are really going to die!"

"We are not! I won't let him kill you!" Bryce growled at the mirror out his door. "Hang on, Eloise. The sun will be up soon."

Soon? I highly doubted that, but I wasn't about to object while he held my life in his steering wheel gripped hands. My eyes were still open wide, and I felt no urge to lay my head down on a pillow. Of course, with the demon horse running behind us, my adrenalin pumped hard. Although…

"He spelled me too, the stupid magician!"

"He did what?" Bryce looked my way.

I pointed to the road. "Don't look away! Duck!"

Bryce lowered his head and we guarded our faces against the glass in time for the horseman to make Bryce's SUV a convertible. I wasn't a fan of the style.

"The magician," I yelled over the wind now hitting us, "the Latin he whispered to you was a spell so you wouldn't sleep tonight so Headless could hunt and kill you. I heard it and haven't fallen asleep all night either. I'm not tired."

Bryce's lips moved, but I couldn't hear what he muttered. The words wouldn't have been nice if I had.

The car swerved to the left and I recognized the welcome sign for Ranger's Ranch ahead when the horse and rider hit our car, sending it skidding in the gravel drive. Bryce had it under control in seconds, but I'd left my stomach back there.

"Where are we going?" We kept accelerating past the lodge and into the fields. I had no idea what the plan was.

"The forest! Be ready to run!"

I held my hand over my seatbelt buckle, not intent to release it until we were near a complete stop. A feeling in my gut said the stop would come fast and my face didn't need more damage from impacting the dashboard.

Our headlights bobbed up and down on the ground in the field. My seatbelt kept me mostly in place on the rough ride as the forest at the end of the field drew closer.

We accelerated with a jerk. Metal crunched. I looked back. Headless had nicked the back of the SUV with his ax, but thanks to Bryce's quick acceleration, we'd been spared.

The SUV swung left. I held onto the seat. With all the belt had been through, I didn't count on it holding out much longer.

"Get ready to run!" Bryce braked hard and the SUV came

to a stop. I released my belt a second too soon when Headless' steed ran into the vehicle and sent me into the dashboard.

Tears stung my eyes and more blood dripped from my nose, but Headless' horse's whinnies woke me from my stupor. He hadn't been fazed by the impact.

Bryce met me at the front of the SUV. I couldn't look around for Headless but the tree he took down with his ax behind me as I pushed into the forest said he was right at my back. This time around, would he leave the horse behind like he had at the lodge? If so, we were in so much trouble.

9

Rain began to pelt us again as Bryce pulled me through the forest. His grip on me wasn't as firm this time because of the water coating our hands, but he kept me up to speed with him. Considering I had to breathe in and out through my mouth and the tears and rain blinded me, he did a fairly good job at keeping us both alive.

Galloping on the left drew attention to a path we hadn't noticed. The horse flew by us, without a rider, and my fear sunk in. Headless was on foot behind us. A killing blow could come at any moment. We'd never see it coming.

The ground beneath our feet began to rise with each step and my heart hurt along with my face at the effort. If I didn't die tonight, tomorrow my muscles would make me wish I had.

"Keep running!" Bryce pulled me along when I stumbled. I didn't have the air or energy to yell back at him that my body was through and I was giving this my all. I mean, I didn't *want* to die.

The air behind my head whistled as the rain lightened. A tree just to my right a few steps back went down, letting me know how close I'd come to losing my head. How could the guy see without a head? Why couldn't he run into trees?

A shriek left my mouth as my foot slipped in the mud. My hand ripped from Bryce's hold as I fell down an embankment on our right. He called my name, but I kept falling. He needed to run now.

Saplings and bigger trees hit me on my way down until a large tree found my stomach and knocked the breath from me. That tree was the one to stop me. Everything hurt and stung from the fall and impact. There'd be no more running for me. Headless' squishy feet in the mud were making their way down the hill to me. Why couldn't he fall in the mud and slide down the hill too? He didn't even have a head!

"El! El, get up!" Bryce's voice cracked with terror, but I couldn't bring myself to do more than roll over onto my back at his words. That hurt enough, but I wanted to see Simmering Simmons one more time before I died.

Headless blocked my view, though. He stood above me, ax in hand. This was it. My bad luck had hit its peak and my time had come.

A thump registered in my ears before the sight of the arrow sticking out of Headless' chest did. Someone had shot the monster with an arrow, but didn't they know it would do no good? Even the sword my father had given me had done nothing to slow Headless down when Bryce had impaled him. It was a nice try, but I was still a dead woman. The sun hadn't risen yet.

"El? El!" Bryce knelt at my side. Why was he here? He should be running.

Headless grabbed at the arrow as he flickered. Flickered?

My injuries were worse than I'd feared, or the pain made me hallucinate.

"Eloise?" Bryce touched my face with the tips of his fingers. His gentleness took my attention from a staggering Headless to the handsome man.

"Bryce," I gasped, but cried out when my ribs screamed in pain.

"Oh, El. Quiet, beautiful. Don't speak. We'll find a way to get you out of here and find some help." He looked around. "Hello? Who's out there?"

"I'm here, kid." An older man with a wooden bow walked into my view. "How is she? That was quite the tumble."

"She's alive, but I don't know if she's broken anything. Ribs maybe?" Bryce looked down on me. "I'll get you out of here alive, El. I promise."

The older man, his white hair reflecting in the moon's light now that the storm had passed, frowned at the monster. Who was he? Where had he come from?

"Pick the girl up and follow me. The phantom won't stay down forever. The herbs on the arrow won't last more than an hour. Even now, he's still dangerous."

Bryce lifted me to place an arm behind my shoulders and I hissed. "Sorry, El. The curse or whatever lasts until the sun rises. Then he'll be gone. At least that's the impression we've been given."

The old man nodded. "Good. The herbs will last that long. Come."

Bryce hefted me into his arms. Poor man. I wasn't light. The pain pushed me in and out of awareness as the two men made their way through the woods. At first, noises behind us indicated Headless wanted to follow, but he couldn't keep up for once.

Whinnies when we reached a flatter path indicated the demon horse was near and my fear spiked.

"Oh settle down, you creature of darkness, or I'll put another arrow in you." The old man's grumble gave way to relief inside me and I relaxed into Bryce again. "If I were young like the two of you, I would have caught up to you sooner. You've been all over the Ranch."

"Yes, sir. We even tried to leave, but the creature and his horse are much faster than a normal horse."

"Black magic will do that to you. Who created this beast?"

"A magician, or that's the role he played tonight at the magic show. One of my dad's employees hired him to kill me. Eloise had the unfortunate experience to be looped into that with me." Bryce kissed my forehead again. "I'm so sorry, El."

"We'll take the girl to my place and I'll do my best to fix her up. She'll need a hospital too when the sun comes up."

"I'll make sure she gets the care she needs."

They continued to talk on their way to Hugh's place. Turned out, Hugh was a druid. He worked in herbs, plants, salts, crystals, oils, and more. If Headless hadn't shown up, I would have continued to doubt real magic existed, but witches, yeah, they were real. Or wizards in the magician's case. Either way, they weren't all bad. Just the ones who dealt in dark magic like Headless' creator. Druids weren't magical in the same way as witches. They worked with the land more instead of through spells.

Hugh also worked at the Ranch. His job was to oversee and manage the stables and trails. I wanted to give the man a hug for coming after us. Five minutes later and I'd be without my head.

Warmth brushed against my skin when Hugh invited Bryce and I into his small home behind the lodge and stables.

"Lay her here."

Bryce lay me on something hard and flat but didn't leave my side. His hand stayed in mine as noises from Hugh's movements came from around the room.

"This will smell bad, but it'll help the pain." Hugh administered something onto my nose wound, and it did stink. I just didn't have the energy to care. While the pain lessened, it never went away.

Next, Hugh applied a concoction that would fight off infection. All the while, Bryce stayed by my side talking to me. My muddled brain couldn't figure out what he was saying, but the tone was comforting.

"The sun will be up soon." Hugh spoke after he'd been quiet for some time when he'd finished bandaging me up. "I'll head over to the lodge and do what I can to fill in what happened to the magician and to you guys. If anyone asks, some crazy guy attacked you in the night along with his friends. They also drugged everyone at the lodge."

"The police will believe that?"

Hugh snorted. "There's a druid on the force. He'll let the story by. I'll also call an ambulance for Ms. Eloise."

"Bryce." My mouth was dry. Water would have been nice, but I'd likely choke on it. "Thank you."

"I didn't do anything but almost get you killed." He pushed some hair out of my face. "I'll make sure you're taken care of, El."

The pain had become manageable and my body, exhausted

now that the no sleeping spell had worn off with the sun, felt heavy and tired. I fell asleep to Bryce's lips on my forehead. I could get used to that.

When I woke, a beeping noise greeted me along with a smell that made my nose crinkle. A very antiseptic smell. The memories came back fast, and I groaned as the pain set in too. I was in a hospital.

"El?" I cracked one eye open to see Zoe beside me in a chair. She didn't wear makeup, her hair wasn't done to perfection, and her face was splotchy from crying. Yet, my bestie still looked like the most beautiful woman on the planet. How unfair was that?

The lights made my eye water, so I closed my eye again but gave Zoe a tired smile. I didn't even have the energy yet to say anything.

"The doctor says you have some cracked ribs and a fractured nose, but other than that you'll be fine. I can't believe you and Simmer got caught up with that guy who demolished your car. No one could believe what he and his gang did to Bryce's SUV. Rumor is, it was some guy mad at Simmer's dad who hired them. Can you believe that?"

Yes, I could. Even if I hadn't heard Nick's confession to Bryce's dad. People had killed or had people killed for less.

"Bryce and his dad are in the waiting room and your parents are on the way. I almost called him Simmer to his face, so I've been trying to call him Mr. Simmons or Bryce now to keep from messing up again. That would have been so embarrassing."

I laughed but stopped right away when my ribs flared up.

"Sorry." Zoe's apology carried a wince with it. "Do you want to see Bryce?"

I managed a small nod. The door opened and closed a few seconds later. I must have nodded off again because a large hand in mine brought me back to reality.

"Zoe said you're awake. Did you fall back asleep on me?"

Again, I smiled, but this time, I forced words out. "Almost."

"I won't keep you awake long. You need your sleep. Plus, your parents just arrived and Zoe's talking to them, so that only gives me a few minutes with you."

I forced my eyes open, blinking against the light in the room. Bryce had dark circles under his eyes and a bruise on his cheek. His hair was tousled, and he had the nerve to look hot that way.

"You need sleep." My voice was deep and gravely, but he only laughed at me.

"I look that great, huh?"

"More than great."

Bryce reached out and cupped my cheek. "That was by far the worst first date I've ever taken a girl on before."

"I didn't like Halloween before. Now, I hate it."

He smiled. "What do you say we try this again sometime, only we watch Christmas movies and cuddle on the couch?"

I smiled with a sigh. "My kinda date."

Bryce chuckled and leaned in. This time, his lips brushed mine instead of my head and if Bryce's gentle kiss with me lying injured in a bed was something to spark my heart rate, I wanted a kiss when I was fully healthy. If everything went according to my plan, I'd have one of those soon. Maybe my bad luck hadn't been so bad after all. Headless wasn't a peach, but I'd gotten the guy in the end.

About Melanie

Melanie's love of writing was instilled in her during the fourth grade when she co-wrote her first sloppily written, hand-drawn, book with her sisters. Since then, she has taken her love of writing to the next level with published novels. Her husband, two sons, and dog, Toby, are her biggest supporters.

MORE FROM MELANIE GILBERT

The Elementals Series

Life and Water

Earth

Air

Lightning

Healing and Love

Fire

The Fae Brothers' Ever Afters Series

Midnight

Enchanted

Captive

Poison

Deal

Deception

Alpha King

The Curse of Thorn

Darkness Untold

Christis Christie

1

Monte Cassino, Latin Valley, Italy - 550 CE

The morning air had held a crispness to it as he'd woken. He was up, and moving about his cell quickly to dress in the rough, brown robes that added a little protection from the elements—but not much. A little misery throughout the day was a good reminder of the penance one owed for the sins of the previous day. As was the hard stone floor beneath his knees while he knelt for his morning prayer and meditations.

Just prior to 6:00am, he had joined the other brothers filing silently into the chapel for morning service. The chanted mass echoed off the stone archways above them. The solemn thrum of their prayers carrying through the abbey never ceased to fill Tommaso with a sense of divine fellowship. Just as their voices were one, they were one with God.

The brothers had broken their fast over gruel made with hearty goat milk and a cask of water to wash it down. Now, Tommaso stooped low in the gardens, basking in the heat of the sunshine as he plucked beans to be dropped into the satchel at his side. One row over, Brother Paolo was doing the same, but there was a hymn upon his lips as he carried out their morning task. Overall, there was a peacefulness to the abbey, even the gardens, with only the occasional hammer or movement of a ladder as several of the brothers worked on re-thatching the roof to the root cellar's exterior entrance.

"Brother Tommaso, I hoped I might have a word with you." The voice coming from over his shoulder belonged to his abbot, Father Cassian.

Wiping his hands clean upon his robes, Tommaso stood and cautiously turned around so as not to trample any of the prospering bean plants. "Of course Father."

Father Cassian motioned for him to leave the garden rows and join him as he began to walk along the green grasses of the monastery's inner grounds. Falling easily into step beside him, Tommaso placed his hands around opposite wrists, allowing the long sleeves of his robe to fall down over them as they walked.

"As you may have noticed of late, Brother Tiberius has aged considerably. God very nearly called him home during his illness last winter, and he has never truly recovered from it. While I wish to respect his life of devoted service to the faith, I do not want to press him onward in duties he is no longer capable of."

Tommaso nodded in understanding, but remained silent at the abbot's side.

"My wish is for Brother Tiberius to step down, and instead focus on daily personal meditations and working however he may in the library. A place no one will notice should he fall asleep." The last part was more of an aside to himself, for Father Cassian cleared his throat before contin-uing on. "However, this means that we have lost our Cantor."

Tommaso, unable to resist, peered over at Father Cassian,

feeling perhaps more excitement than was proper for what he hoped the abbot was getting to.

"While I had my own thoughts on the matter, I have spoken to a number of others, as well as Brother Tiberius himself, and we have all agreed that you are the perfect candidate to take over leadership of the choir." At this point, Father Cassian ceased in his steps and turned to face Tommaso. While he was shorter than Tommaso, there was a firm, confident air to the abbot's gaze that could pin any of the brothers in their place.

"I…am honoured to be considered," Tommaso began, his pulse thrumming in his throat. He had loved music even in his youth. The wandering bards who occasionally passed through his small village always a spot of excitement, and thrill.

"It is a role that comes with much responsibility, Tommaso, and must be seen to with a sense of heavenly devotion, and fealty. When our choir raises their voice, they sing not just for the pleasure of those listening, but with the intent of reaching the ears of God, and His Son upon their heavenly thrones. It is out of praise of the Holy Trinity, and much needed prayer that we commune in such a way. As Cantor, it will be your duty to lead the choir on this most sacred of paths. Are you ready for that responsibility?" Father Cassian gazed back at him with a solemn expression.

Tommaso felt the excitement within him level out as the weight of great responsibility fell to his shoulders. He was young as a brother yet, and to be gifted such a role was an incredible honour.

"I am humbled Father, and while I am weak in my own right, I will depend upon the guidance of the Lord to aid me in the new duty of Cantor." His voice was low, but steady as he responded.

Father Cassian nodded. "I have every faith that you will."

554 CE

Arms lifted in the air, Tommaso led the choir through the hymns for the evening mass, as well as the evening passage. They had been practicing for several hours this afternoon and would break only for the evening meal, before heading to the chapel for mass. The voices of the brothers before him rose in a solemn manner that not only echoed off the stone walls, but reverberated deep within him. Nothing had fulfilled him so greatly as the role of Cantor had. Leading his brothers down a closer path to God through the means of song, had given him deeper appreciation for the gifts their Heavenly Father had bestowed upon them.

As they came to the final verse, his hands gently drew out the last chords before closing with a flick. The voices ceased, only the faint ring off the walls an indication of what had been.

"Well done, brothers. You may retire until dinner is called." At his words, the monks before him began to file out, but he caught the eye of one young brother, and motioned for him to stay behind.

"Yes, Brother Tommaso?" he questioned, coming to stand before him.

"You're holding back," Tommaso stated, gazing back at the young lad.

Ezra had only joined the order a short six months before. While studious and earnest in his newly minted vow, there was most evidently a part of himself that he was still afraid to give.

"I…" The boy frowned, his confusion flickering over his features. "Aren't I meant to?"

Tommaso smiled and reached out to rest his hand on his shoulder in a comforting manner. "Walk with me," he instructed.

The two fell in step alongside each other as they began a slow trek towards the end of the abbey where the dining hall lay.

"The life that each of us has chosen is one of simplicity and quiet reflections, and I can see how that would seem conflicting in nature. We lead this life so that nothing stands in the way of our connection to God, nor interrupts our time of meditation. However…" He smiled over at the boy as he spoke. "Our praise should never be simple, or restrained. Do not be afraid to take pleasure in your singing, or to lose yourself to the chant. Our song is holy, and while we sing for Him, we also sing for ourselves. We sing of our love, and our devotion, and one should never be ashamed of taking pleasure in that. Or of feeling all that it has to offer."

There was silence as they walked, only the soft tread of their sandals upon the floor, and Ezra mulled over his words. Tommaso gave him the time to think it through, and let his heart and his head settle on the truth of them. It was a journey of knowledge and acceptance that each new brother had to take—a life of solitude, and simplicity, did not mean cutting oneself off from all great, and true emotions.

"Thank you, I believe I understand what you are saying," Brother Ezra spoke at last. "We should not close ourselves off from the immense love and joy God gives us, in any form that it may come."

Tommaso smiled gently, and nodded. "Precisely. Now, go take your seat. We don't want to be late for the blessing."

Evening had fallen upon the abbey, and while most of the brothers had retired to their cells for the night, Tommaso found himself wandering down one of the lone corridors alongside the open courtyard. Though he had now spent almost half of his life here, the moments just after night mass could still fill his bones with a restlessness begging to be walked out before he was able to find ease of sleep.

The abbey was silent, only the moon above filtering in through the high arches of the corridor to accompany him on his stroll. His thoughts mulled over the evening mass, and the difference in Brother Ezra's countenance he had witnessed. There had definitely been a new-found lightness to the way that he sang. It filled Tommaso with happiness to think he had helped him find some inner peace.

As he passed the large stone basin that held the holy water in the midst of their courtyard, a shriek of pain and terror broke the peaceful silence around him. It was enough to make him stumble in his steps and pause, his heart beating an erratic tempo in his chest. The cry did not come again, but it had sounded from somewhere near the entrance to the courtyard, and without delay, Tommaso began to run in that direction, as fast as his robes would allow him.

Chest heaving with exertion as he darted out into the courtyard and made his way in the darkness, he sent up a silent prayer that whomever had made that terrible noise was okay. His steps faltered once more as he came upon the large stone entrance. There, in the shadows beneath the arch, a body lay crumpled on the ground with another hulking presence bent over it, arms clutching the unmoving form to its chest.

"Stop! What are you doing?" Tommaso cried, the scene before him confusing, and obscene.

His shout seemed to rouse the bent form and its head lifted. A pale face was half-shielded by darkness. Its mouth was visible, lips stained with red that dripped just a little at their edges. Startled more, Tommaso stopped entirely, his eyes dropping from the ravenous beast before him to the figure that lay within its arms. The boy's head had fallen to the side, exposing the torn flesh along the column of his throat and the sightless eyes that stared up at the sky.

"Ezra!" Tommaso gasped out, stomach turning, and body chilling at the lifeless form of his fellow brother. "What have you done!?" The scream tore from his throat. Sanity was replaced by anger and pain as he lunged for the creature

Bodies colliding, the force sent the cloaked being backwards, and Tommaso along with it. Together they rolled, Tommaso grappling for a hold of the creature's garments to try and restrain it in some measure. However, the form was like that of stone and, in due time, had Tommaso entirely pinned beneath it.

In the closeness of their bodies, he was able to see that the being above him wore the semblance of a man: shockingly blue eyes, pale features framed by coifs of golden curls, and a face that would have been cherubic, if not for the piercing, white fangs peeking from beneath a snarling lip.

"Demon!" he gasped, breath ragged.

"And so much more," was the returning snarl, before the beast sunk its fangs deeply into Tommaso's throat. His scream of pain echoed out into the silence of the night sky.

Above, the moon watched. Silent. Distant.

Tommaso slowly regained consciousness—mind hazy, throat parched, and a desperate need for sustenance overtaking him. Gradually, flickers of memory returned, and his hand went frantically to his throat as his eyes opened. Darkness greeted him and yet, he could make out—in fine detail—the rocks of the cave above him. At his pulse, his fingers found no evidence of any harm done. In fact, his body felt entirely whole and unmarred.

Sitting up, Tommaso glanced around him. While still in his brown robes, which even in darkness he could tell were torn and stained, he was nowhere on the grounds of the monastery. How was he still alive? The last, most vivid thing he could remember was a white-fanged demon bearing down upon him and tearing into the flesh of his neck. Yet, as his fingers had belied, there was no wound to be found.

The stifling nature of the cave began to weigh upon him and, with an uncertain grasp, he reached to rest his hand on the stone wall, pulling himself up. His legs felt strange and unfamiliar, each step a little gangly and uncoordinated, like a new calf learning to walk for the first time. Though it wasn't weakness making them so, but an uneasy strength that overpowered him. Despite this, he found himself at the mouth of the cave in short order, peering out on a sleeping landscape of hills and a valley dotted with cottages.

Recognition dawned on him. He knew the rolling hills with the small farm nestled between them—his home. There, in the lower fields of the valley stood a little house with a small barn, and inside rested his parents. He had lived with them, his older brother, and two younger sisters, until he was fifteen, at which point his parents had deemed him ready to join the brothers in the abbey in Monte Cassino.

"Mother," he whispered. Even his voice sounded foreign to his ears. Too loud, too crisp, a melody of thunder in the softest of pleas.

Tommaso moved without thought, single-minded intent guiding him down the hillside toward the memories of his childhood. It had been five years since his parents had last paid a visit to the abbey, just a brief stop on their way to Rome and his brother Eduardo and family. A pang of longing filled him, driving away any doubt. At this confusing time, home was where he should be.

Despite the moonless night, Tommaso made his way over the grassy knolls quickly and without trouble, his gaze fixated on the small farm. The house itself was dark and silent, telling him that everyone was fast asleep. It was eerie, to be approaching his childhood home in the dead of the night, the world around him unresponsive to his presence.

At the front door his hand halted in midair while his mind contemplated the repercussions of waking his parents from their sleep. And yet, his underlying hunger pushed him on. Something innately instinctual was telling him if he didn't have food soon, he may very well go mad.

Hand trembling, he rapped firmly the door, then braced himself with both hands upon the wooden frame, head hung low as he waited. Through the quiet of the night, Tommaso heard the distinct sound of his father speaking, voice muffled, but carrying to him. Eyes shut, he could picture his movements through the house, hearing each step and shift. As he neared the door, a light thumping noise captured Tommaso's ear more intently than anything else. He felt his hunger increase, and a craving filled his gut and took over his being.

As the door opened, his head lifted, dark eyes meeting the matching set in his father's shocked expression. At the same time as his father was comprehending the sight before him, Tommaso was hit by a scent so unbelievably delicious he thought he might go mad without it. The doorframe beneath his tightening hands creaked in protest.

"Maso? What are you do—is that blood? Are you okay!?" his father exclaimed, concern lacing each word as he reached a hand out to him.

"Father...I don't know what's happened," he responded, once again his voice sounding both the same, and different to his own ears.

Setting aside the candle in his hand, his father grasped his side and pulled him forward, while his other hand began to search over his form. Tommaso realized the stains on his robe were actually dried blood, not merely dirt as he had initially presumed.

His body straining, seeking to be satiated, Tommaso inhaled deeply to calm the hunger inside of him—it had the opposite effect. As he drew in a breath, the favourable scent in the air rolled over his tongue, igniting a beast within. Shock flashed through him as two sharp points pricked at his bottom lip, and Tommaso felt every cell inside of his body focused upon a single point on his father's throat—a pulsing rhythm dancing along with the thumping noise echoing inside his head.

Before either of them registered what was happening, Tommaso was upon his father. His arms encircled his older frame and pulled him tightly against his chest. His father struggled, but his frail human form was nothing against the newfound strength inside Tommaso's arms tightening around him with crushing force. A haze of ravenous hunger drove him forward, and as his teeth punctured the tender flesh at his father's throat, a coppery ambrosia coursed over his tongue.

A muffled cry of pain and terror escaped his father's lips, resonating deeply within Tommaso. Yet, the awakened beast could not be stopped, not with blood now flowing past his lips. Each drop was embodied with the taste of life, and sweet notes of fear—an addictive medley he could not cease drinking until every last, precious drop had been guzzled down.

The blood was intoxicating, painting his mind with a veil of red as he allowed the slack form in his arms to slip to the floor. In doing so, he became aware of the other presence in the room, a scream of confusion piercing through the fog enough to draw his gaze. Her fear was a heady scent upon the air, coiling about him like inviting fingers, pulling him forward. In a few, quick strides he was upon her, her wailing palms upon his chest and shoulders mere taps of annoyance. The unquenchable thirst for blood still clouding his thoughts, his hand fisted in her hair, yanking her head back to expose her throat.

Dark eyes latched upon the frantic pulse in the column of

her neck and he lashed out, biting into that pulse in a desperate need to devour the very essence of the life within his stone clutch. She whimpered in agony, a sound that settled at the centre of his heart and took root there as he swallowed each mouthful of coppery delight in a gluttonous manner.

When it was over, Tommaso sunk to his knees on the floor, falling back upon his heels. In his arms his mother lay, her head nestled gently upon his chest, his fingers wound through her grey streaked locks. At her throat was the garish proof of his betrayal.

All life now decimated within the residence, the beast inside of Tommaso slackened its hold and slipped back into the recesses of his mind, taking with it the red haze of desperate hunger. In its wake, Tommaso was left with nothing but the deafening silence of his childhood home, and the pale corpses of his parents. A broken sob of horror forced itself from deep within him, and he clutched his mother's lifeless form to his chest, burying his face in her hair to avoid the heartbroken look of despair and accusation within her eyes.

What had become of him in the depths of that cave? There was a demon residing within him, one that had full control of his entire body, mind and soul. His shoulders shook with the strength of his misery as he held on to the remainder of his beloved mother, feeling her body grow cold in his arms.

How did he get the demon out?

His parents had deserved a proper burial, but Tommaso feared the repercussions of being killed by a demon. Reciting a prayer—that he was no longer worthy to say—in hopes of speeding their souls on to God, Tommaso then threw the oil lantern to the floor and tossed his father's discarded candle into the puddle. The blaze burned hot and angry within seconds, eager flames licking along floorboards and quickly engulfing his mother. Stepping away, Tommaso slipped back into the darkness of the moonless night, leaving behind the fire spreading through the farmhouse, and bid farewell to the happiness of his past.

Tommaso knew no other place to turn to, than back to the brothers in the abbey. If anyone would know how to exorcise the demon clutching his soul, it would be Father Cassian.

He didn't make it back to the abbey before sunrise. As the first rays began to crest the hillside Tommaso felt searing agony raking his over his skin, the very rays of the sun dragging upon his flesh. With little choice in the matter, he ducked into the first barn he could find, hiding in the darkest depths it afforded. He was filled with fear at the thought he would do harm to the livelihood of this poor family. Or, should one of the members of this household stumble upon him the beast would take over yet again, and more would die.

However, as he concealed his form with straw, Tommaso found a much-needed sleep washing over him and, without consent, sunk into the oblivion of it.

Night had fallen when he woke at last, the rested wonder of his body a direct contrast to the torment of his thoughts. Though the memories of his own attack at the abbey were still clouded, the sight of his parents' bloodless corpses strewn upon the floor were emblazoned upon his mind.

Concerned for the welfare of the family who lived on this land, as much as for the state of his own soul, Tommaso broke a portion of the barn board wall and snuck out behind the building, slinking into the darkness, and away. He had made it through the day without mishap, if only he could make it to the abbey without staining his hands with more death.

The hunger and thirst had returned, clawing at his throat and causing his jaw to ache, but Tommaso pushed on, forcing each step to take him closer to the abbey at Monte Cassino. Though his determination had zeroed in on the road before him, Tommaso did not realize how quickly his steps had taken him over the countryside until he was at the base of the mountain and looking up at the winding road that would take him to the woods around the monastery. The night was barely half over, and he found himself not in the least winded, or tired.

It was the throbbing hunger pulsing at his teeth and gnawing at his insides that was the true sign of his exertion. The demon within him was craving more of the divine elixir that flowed through the veins of those around him. Somehow, Tommaso would need to restrain it long enough for Father Cassian to cast it away. The last thing he wanted was a recurrence of his family home.

3

With trepidation and a dwindling grasp on hope, Tommaso made the journey up the mountainside, coming upon the front gates of the abbey before he was truly ready. Momentarily, he paused on the cusp of stepping through the arch, wondering if the devil's spawn wrapped around his soul would keep him from stepping upon such hallowed ground—it did not.

The grounds were silent, the brothers having retired to their rooms for evening prayers and needed sleep. Tommaso found himself missing the simplicity of his cell, the chill of stone rooms that would settle onto his form and make it all the easier to crawl beneath the covers of his bed and sleep the night away. He longed for the hardness of the floor beneath his knees as he prayed, and the scent of the straw-filled mattress at his nose.

Where once he had felt at home in these holy walls, Tommaso now felt like a trespasser, tarnished by sin and disgrace. Entering the wing of the abbey that housed the brothers' chambers, he felt his throat constrict with need, and the prick of sharp fangs at his bottom lip. Each door he passed echoed with the tempting sound of the lazy heartbeats of his sleeping brethren. It was only the closed doors between them that kept the beast at bay, and enabled him to make it to the third floor where Father Cassian's rooms were.

He wanted to knock, to warn him that he was there, but something stopped his hand in the process of rising. Instead, his fingers dropped to circle around the door latch, and slowly he pushed the door open.

Inside, the room was dark. Tommaso could hear the steady breathing of Father Cassian, and the soft rhythm of his heart. Without thought, his tongue darted out to moisten his lips as he swallowed against the tide of hunger rising inside him.

"Father…" He called softly into the darkness, his eyes following the slow rise and fall of the older man's chest beneath the heavy covers of his bed.

It took a moment for his voice to register, but gradually Father Cassian woke. Even in the darkness of the room, Tommaso was able to see him blink away his drowsiness.

"Father," Tommaso called once more.

This time, Father Cassian sat up, startled, his heart rate increased, the tempo like drums of war to Tommaso's ears— calling him to action. His teeth ached now, they wanted so badly to sink into the flesh at the abbot's throat, and it took all his strength to restrain himself. If he remained perfectly still and did not inhale, perhaps the beast would not be released.

"Who's there?" The older man shifted, throwing away the bedding and resting his feet upon the wooden floorboards. It took a moment for his eyes to adjust to the darkness and, when they did, he squinted, gazing at the space where Tommaso stood. "Tommaso? Is that you?"

There was confusion in the abbot's voice, which did not surprise Tommaso, who knew what they had thought became of him. "Yes, Father, it is me."

"Where have you been? We thought you had been lost." Father Cassian stood to his feet, moving in his night clothes to grasp a candle, which after a quick strike of a flint, sparked to life. Picking up the holder, he stepped over to him, but stopped when Tommaso held up his hand to halt him.

"Don't," he gasped raggedly, the scent of the other man beginning to tease his nostrils. "Don't come any closer."

Father Cassian's eyes fell over Tommaso's form, taking in his filthy robes, and the dark stains upon the coarse wool before lifting to look at his face. His features had paled, and the abbot quickly made the sign of the cross over himself.

"May God have mercy…Tommaso… What has become of you?" Horror sounded in his voice and quivered in his eyes. He did not come any closer.

"I think I've been possessed, Father." His voice quaked with barely restrained emotions. He was frightened—for himself, and of himself. "Brother Ezra was slain, and the beast that did so attacked me when I tried to stop it. Please, you have to help me be rid of this thing inside me before I hurt someone else."

There was silence in the room as Father Cassian gazed back at him, the horror now mixing with sadness. The elderly monk began to shake his head gently. Tommaso felt his hands tighten at his sides, the hunger that had brimmed below the surface now at the boiling point, rumbling inside him and desperate to be fed. Red threatened to coat his vision once more, but he fought against it, his chest heaving with unneeded breath, which only intensified the scents surrounding him.

"Please help me," he begged softly.

"I am sorry my son, but I cannot," Father Cassian spoke gently.

"But, you must!" He could feel tears of devastation pooling beneath his lids. The abbot was his only hope.

"I cannot," he returned once more. "Brother Ezra was slain by a vile creature without hope, one of the damned. Vampyr."

Tommaso shook his head, denying it. Creatures of such name did not exist, they were naught but stories to frighten children into coming home before the wild animals of the night could harm them.

"Please, you're the only one who can save me. You need to exorcize the demon from me, please."

Father Cassian moved over to the desk at the side of the room, retrieving a small rectangular box from the depths of it.

"You do not carry within you a demon that can be exorcized…You *are* one of the damned. You have bonded with the demon Tommaso." There was a deep sadness within Father Cassian's voice as he spoke, a finality to his words. "There is no hope for you now, but the quick and merciful strike of an ash stake through your heart."

The abbot turned slowly to face him. Within his grasp he held a long piece of wood, shaved down to a bone-piercing point at one end. Tommaso felt his insides revolt at the notion he was beyond saving, that the demon within him was not a being striving to take control, but his own nature.

"No," he protested.

Slowly, Father Cassian came towards him, like a man approaching a snake about to strike. "There is no other way." His statement was followed by the soft chanting of a prayer

Tommaso recognized. Father Cassian was praying for his soul, whatever may be left of it.

If he had been a truly decent person, he would have closed his eyes and allowed the blow to come, ending whatever terror he had already inflicted upon the world. His hands had other ideas. Father Cassian came at him quickly, a cross raised in one hand and the stake in the other, his Latin prayer spilling out rapidly. Tommaso caught his wrist in the air on its descent, crushing the fragile bones which caused the abbot to drop the stake to the floor with a clatter.

"Tommaso—" he began, bringing the cross up to press to his cheek. It did nothing, except annoy the monster inside him.

They were too close, and Father Cassian had intended harm towards him. What little restraint Tommaso had over himself slipped. As the red haze swam over his vision entirely, he knew that when this was over, there would be more death upon his hands.

He lost count of how many died, the bloodthirsty monster inside him having taken over entirely. Tommaso became lost to himself and the taste of blood flowing so freely over his tongue. When it was over, he knelt upon the steps of the abbey, his robes soaked through and his body satiated for the first time since he had woken in the darkness of that cave—a monster born from death and blood.

There was still movement in the abbey, he could hear the cries of horror and shock as the bodies were discovered by those who remained. He could not stay here, but he had no place to go and daybreak would be upon him soon enough. With little thought of what to do, Tommaso left the final body he had drained—another of the younger brothers who'd thought to stop the monster before it could escape—and walked solemnly across the courtyard, passing the holy water basin as he did so.

It crossed his mind to stop and douse himself with it, see if it would perhaps burn away the evil, stripping him down to whatever was left. Instead, he carried himself out the gates of the Monte Casino abbey, and wandered deep into the woods. When he was far enough away that he could no longer hear the screams, but only the distant ringing of the warning bells, he knelt upon the forest floor and began to dig. He dug until there was a hole wide enough and deep enough to encase him, and then he slipped into it. Pulling the soil over him, Tommaso successfully buried himself within the dank earth and found himself wishing it truly was his grave that he lay in.

Perhaps it was the added shade of the trees, or the fact he had fully covered himself with soil, but Tommaso did not wake from his death like sleep until the sun had set. He woke to find himself whole and unscathed. It wasn't fair, nor was it right.

Damned, without hope, and with too much blood on his hands to ever wash away, Tommaso didn't even try to fight the beast inside him when it reared its hungry head. Instead he followed the scent of fresh blood to a small cabin in the woods. He couldn't enter the cabin, something held him back at the threshold, but his hunger pushed him forward. When he called out to the man and woman who lived inside, Tommaso felt a connection form between himself and the couple, a bond that allowed him to feel their emotions to twist and contort them.

Once they beckoned him in, he found all hesitation at the doorstep gone, and soon he fell upon them, feasting until the hollow feeling inside him disappeared.

4

The rain was heavy on the dark streets as Tommaso slunk through the shadows. His cloak was sodden and clinging to his shoulders, trailing through puddles, as bare feet slapped against dirt and stone. Travelling the roads to Cordoba, sustenance had been hard to come by; his hunger was now at a ravenous stage that made him more prone to risky behaviours. This life of hunting and feeding in the night was one of stealth and secrecy, lest he expose himself to the church, who would surely put a stake through his heart as Father Cassian had desired those many years before.

While there was a dark, self-loathing undercurrent to everything Tommaso did, there was also a strong fervour for life. It had kept him in the shadows, hiding where none would ever know he existed, and leaving quickly before the trail of death could be traced back to him.

Tonight, he was not thinking of stealth, nor of secrecy. He was following the most delicious scent that had chased away any conscientious thought of caution. Dark hair already plastered to his face, Tommaso pushed his hood back and allowed the rain to land directly on his head. Drops collected in his hair only to stream down over his forehead. Long lashes gathered together in sharp spikes over his dark brown eyes, which were locked upon the figure moving quickly between the empty market stalls ahead.

Tommaso did not know the reason for the figure being out in this godforsaken weather, only that the blood pumping through their veins called to him. Having found the source of the divine scent, he moved more quickly, his bare feet taking him up to them in seconds. Grabbing the person by one arm, he tore off their hood to expose a young woman, fear in her eyes as she peered back and screamed.

Not allowing her youthfulness to stop him, Tommaso used his free hand to take a fistful of auburn hair and pull her head to the side, exposing the vulnerable expanse of neck. Biting into her did not silence the cries of pain and fear, but did begin to satiate the hunger clawing at his insides. Greedily gulping down each mouthful, their bodies gradually sunk to the ground below them. Her cries became whimpers, and the hand once beating at his side now clung to his drenched cloak.

Before he could have his fill, strong hands fell upon them, and tore Tommaso from his prey, tossing him effortlessly across the market to land upon his back in the mud. Panting not from need, but surprise, he pushed himself up. A dirty hand swiped matted hair out of his eyes as he watched the figure leaning over the young woman's body. An unnatural hiss escaped Tommaso's curled lips as the scent of something not-quite human reached him.

"She's mine!" he roared, teeth still sharp and aching to

finish what he had begun. The hunger inside had been denied for far too long.

The other man looked back at him, shooting him a silencing glare across the divide between. "Hush you fool, have you not made enough infernal racket? Do you seek to expose us to all of Cordoba?"

The male, whose shoulder length dark hair was tied together at the nape of his neck, brought his hand to his mouth, pricking his fingertip on a sharp fang which he then swiped over the wounds on the girl's neck. Staggering to his feet and moving closer, Tommaso watched as the puncture wounds healed over, and left her unmarred. Then, without even a blink of remorse, the other man snapped her neck, leaving her lifeless on the ground as he stood back up, pulling the hood of his cloak up over his head.

"Why did you…" Tommaso began, only to falter.

"You cannot leave the body of a victim in the midst of a well-populated area, with marks upon her throat that lead humans directly to us. Now, come with me before we are both discovered." There was only command within his tone, and Tommaso found himself unable to refuse, despite the thirst of hunger still pulsating within him.

The girl had been enough to sate his stomach, but not to fully quench his need. Yet, he pulled the hood of his own cloak up over his head and followed the stranger down through barren allies until they reached a doorway set inside a stone wall.

Alkaios was a Grecian man who lived in a well-established villa within the walls of Cordoba. His garments were of the finest fabrics, and his countenance and bearing that of someone born into a family of influence. He gave little time for Tommaso to think. Instead, once inside the sanctuary of his home, he took Tommaso's cloak from him, and sent him into a small side room to change into a pair of spare trousers and a fresh tunic.

Now he sat before a roaring fire in one of the common rooms, feeling more put together with the rain and mud wiped away. He had finger-combed his dark hair, which was shaggy and unkempt, falling about his proud cheeks and tickling along his angular jaw. It was something he hadn't put much thought into. At the abbey, their heads had been clean shaven, and his hair had only returned after the demon had attacked him. Now, living through each day seemed of more value than the state of his appearance. Yet something about this man, and his home, spoke of propriety which Tommaso had thought he'd well and truly left behind.

Having changed as well, Alkaios brought a tray into the room, set it down on a small table beside his chair, then proceeded to hand Tommaso one of the goblets from it. Inside, he was shocked to find a dark, crimson liquid which made him gaze at Alkaios in surprise.

"You are wondering how I've come by blood in my home, in the middle of the night," Alkaios murmured while taking his own seat, as if reading his mind. "There are less obvious means of doing so, without informing an entire population of your presence amongst it. I have lived here for five years without detection." He took a sip from his goblet, his tongue capturing a wayward droplet from his lips as he set it back down in his lap.

Unable to restrain himself, Tommaso lifted the goblet and gulped down the fragrant blood, a hint of honey accompanying it. When he was done, he wiped the back of his hand over his mouth and found Alkaios watching him with a dark look in his eyes.

"When were you made?" he questioned, his own glass still sitting in his lap. Tommaso found his eyes upon it, thinking of the dark liquid that was safely nestled there inside the bronze.

"554," he responded, having no clear inclination to the present date.

"Seventy years…And you've learned nothing of self-restraint or culling the bloodlust." Alkaios clicked his tongue disapprovingly. "Did your sire teach you naught of control?"

"Sire?" Tommaso frowned, uncertain of whom he was alluding to.

"The vampyr that made you into what you are now," Alkaios clarified.

The frown upon Tommaso's features hardened into something dark, and dangerous. Untouched feelings of anger and pain rose once more to the surface. "The monster who damned me to this life of hell left me to wake alone in a cave near my parents' home and never returned for me," he snarled, hatred dripping from his tongue.

His host scoffed in disgust at this news, drinking from his goblet once more. He then leaned forward to hand the rest to Tommaso, which he accepted greedily, without protest. Resting forward, elbows on his knees, Alkaios gazed upon him intently.

"There are those among the vampyr families who fear we are not reproducing naturally at a speed which the continuation of our race demands. As an immortal race, I've no idea what it is they fear…However, because of this, some have taken it upon themselves to choose humans from among us to transform, rather than waiting for more to be born. In their haste to do so, they are often leaving the fledglings on their own, near vulnerable places they hope will cause them to frenzy feed, and then turn more."

Having downed the remainder of what was in Alkaios' glass, Tommaso found himself staring at the other man in astonishment. He was speaking as if there were creatures out there, other demons such as themselves, who were having children in the natural sense of the word. Yet, there was nothing natural about what he was saying.

"Born?" was all he found it in himself to say.

Alkaios nodded. "Yes, born. Some of us have always been vampyr, and can trace our lineage back to the very first to walk the earth."

"No." Tommaso was shaking his head. "God would not allow such an unnatural thing to occur."

"God has no place in this, fledgling. Our origins are of a darker sort."

"Easy…easy… Maso!" Alkaios shouted, ripping him from the blood haze that had settled

upon him. "Remember what I said, you must drink only until you hear the heart begin to weaken, and then you must stop. This is about control, not killing."

Tommaso lifted his head, panting from the exertion of

stopping himself in the feed. In his arms lay a naked concubine, young and supple. She had sated first one hunger raging within him, and then offered her throat unknowingly, to sate another.

"But, she is an undesirable—" He was cut off with a stern look from Alkaios.

"That is not the point of this instruction, now is it?" His dark coils of hair fell in soft layers about his face, and down to his shoulders. Along his jaw, a shadow had been allowed to grow, giving the handsome features before him a sense of roguish appeal which was only emphasized by the sultry look always there in the depths of his light green eyes.

"No," Tommaso murmured, bowing his head in submission. He bit the top of his thumb so that he could press his healing blood to the wounds in the young concubine's throat.

"Good. She must be left with only the memory of having fed the hunger of our loins, her body offering no indication otherwise. That is how we feed and sustain ourselves, how we keep our place in society undetected." He reached out to smooth Tommaso's hair back from his face, his own straight locks now trimmed and neat, but still long enough to fall into his eyes. "As for the rest…When the desire for a blood bath overtakes you, even then you must cover your tracks." He wiped away a droplet of blood from the corner of Tommaso's mouth, bringing it to his own lips to taste.

"Of course, Aios." Tommaso nodded. It was not his desire to bring ruin down on the man who had taken him into his home, and taught him the truth about himself.

"Now, wake her, and give her the memories you wish her to have." Alkaios stood up, his bronze flesh glowing in the dull lamplight inside the girl's chambers.

He stepped over to a young man, half-drunk and half-glamoured into compliance. Situating himself on a mound of cushions beside him, he pulled the lad into his lap, biting into his throat as he locked eyes with Tommaso. At his side, a young woman stirred, making her way over to Alkaios and his snack on hand and knee. She slipped a hand between the two, fingers exploring bare flesh with intent.

$$5$$

1191 CE Paris, France.

A supple maid sat perched in his lap, feeding him bits of pork from her fingertips which he took as offered, despite them tasting like ash in his mouth. Though his body had ceased requiring such sustenance long ago, and anything ingested now would need to be brought up later, appearances must be maintained. So, as another juicy peace of roasted pork was brought up to his lips, Tommaso accepted it with grace, his eyes meeting those of the young woman as he purposefully grazed her fingers with his teeth while doing so. He watched the responsive shiver travel through her body, and noted the slight elevation in her breathing.

"Maso, how is it your name speaks of Italy, but your voice has no hint of your homeland?" Marie asked in a breathy tone, her hazel eyes silently offering what her body had been all evening.

"I have not lived there in many years," he murmured in response, his own gaze taking him away from her face and to the room at large instead.

Across the great hall Alkaios had gathered a small harem of beautiful and willing supplicants of all shapes, sizes and sexes. It was always the same, no matter where they went. His aura was an allure many could not resist, and Tommaso was certain any number of them would be joining them back in their guest chambers once the banquet had concluded. However, none of them would be calling it a night until King Philip had retired for the evening, and His Royal Highness seemed in no hurry to end the celebrations for his return from the crusades.

King Philip was deep in the spirits, and it would seem the whole of the court had followed suit with frequent laughter, riotous conversation, and a continuous flow of wine. Tommaso found himself embittered by it. A sea of sordid souls partaking in gluttony and lasciviousness to their hearts' content, all morality a thing forgotten until the morrow's façades were slid back into place.

As he fought to stave off the frown of displeasure, he was reminded of Alkaios' words. "*We are here to feed upon the dregs of this life, who waste away what is at their fingertips. Do not regret ending what was not valued, or has been tainted.*"

Marie had moved on from the morsels of pork, and instead was busying herself attending to the column of his throat and the lobe of his ear, her lips pressing soft kisses to the flesh she found within her reach. His own hand slid beneath the layers of her skirt, slipping over stocking clad knees to tickle at bare thighs. She offered him a breathy moan of encouragement.

Tommaso continued to slowly gaze around the room. His dark eyes taking in each drunken body with only mild interest, until they fell upon a slender form seated at the end of the banqueting table, looking aloof and displeased. Beside her, an older gentleman sat, reclining in his seat and looking near ready to spill out of it. His hand was upon the bottom of the maid pouring him more wine as he whispered into her ear.

While he watched the scene, the displeased maiden raised her head and locked eyes with him—they were blue, and as cold as a winter's pond. Her brown hair, which was pulled away from her face and bound together at the top, with the rest left to fall about her shoulders and back, looked like molten honey to his eyes. The rosy glow of blood beneath her cheeks, gave her a look of youthful vitality that caused his fangs to prick his bottom lip.

She must have read something of the hunger in his eyes, for she turned her head away, purposefully breaking eye contact and denying him a vision that would have stolen his breath had he still need of it.

"M'lord, am I not pleasing to you?" Marie whispered, a lilt of distress to her voice.

Returning his attention to the maid in his lap, Tommaso gave a gentle shake of his head in response. "No, sweet one, you are very pleasing, indeed."

He pressed a soft kiss to her lips, feeling her melt into his chest in happiness. The hand upon her thigh slid higher, teasing at warm flesh as he pressed soft kisses along her jaw and down her throat until he was at her pulse. Capturing her flesh gently between his teeth, he worshipped her with his fingertips as he pierced her neck, eliciting a mingled gasp of pain and pleasure from between her lips.

He drank only enough to stave off hunger rather than fill himself, and then pricked his tongue with his tooth so that he could swipe his blood upon the spots on her throat, healing her wounds. Lifting his head, he pressed another kiss to her lips, capturing her panting breath as her pleasure-filled form leaned against his chest. Smoothing her skirts back into place, Tommaso rested a hand upon her waist, and pulled back to look upon her features. She was flushed and pliant, ready to go wherever he would beckon. However, he'd had his fill of her.

"Thank you for your attention, you may return to your duties now," he murmured. Out of the corner of his eye he noticed the maiden from the end of the table standing up to leave with the older gentleman beside her.

Marie protested, but he shook his head, and with his mind told her to leave without complaint. With a distant look in her eyes and a shallow nod of her head, the maid slid off his lap and walked away without another word. Standing, Tommaso made his way across the great hall, feeling Alkaios' calculating eyes upon him as he did. This did not stop him. Curiosity had grasped hold of him, and Tommaso felt a deep yearning to know more of the young maiden with the cold, unhappy eyes.

Laughter followed him out of the banquet hall. A chorus of song taken up by a group of drunken knights echoed off the walls, and he felt the silence of the outer halls welcome him into their embrace. The dark-haired maiden walked before him, just a step or two behind the slovenly nobleman who had brought the serving girl with him—an accommodating, yet unwilling participant in his fondling attentions.

Tommaso quickened his silent tread and, when he was close enough, he reached out a hand to capture the maiden's wrist, and tug her to a firm, yet gentle halt. Spinning towards him, her face showed first surprise, then recognition, before finally ending on disapproval. Wishing to stem whatever tide of unhappy phrases were about to burst from her lips, he began to speak.

"Why do you follow a man old enough to be your grandfather, who has no qualms with groping another woman before your very eyes?" he questioned, searching those blue depths for an answer.

Her eyes, if possible, became even colder than they were in the banqueting hall. "And why do you seek to take that which is not yours?" With a sharp tug, she pulled her wrist free of his loose grasp.

"I meant no offence, but only wished to—"

"To comment on that which you know nothing of, in order to proposition me with a better offer." She cut him off before he could continue. "Let me be perfectly clear, I have no desire to spend my night in your, or anyone else's bed." Her words were a cold whip of ice, striking a fatal blow to any further conversation.

"Manette!" Came a bellow from down the hall, the drunken man now aware she was no longer behind him as he reached the stone steps leading to the guest area of the palace.

"I am coming," she called back. Without another glance in Tommaso's direction, she hurried to catch up with him and the serving girl.

Tommaso felt a hand upon his shoulder, ceasing any efforts to follow after her further. He watched her disappear up the stairs, before turning to Alkaios behind him.

"Why have you left your adoring lovers?" Tommaso asked, feeling like a child about to be scolded for misbehaviour.

"I was curious why my Maso was scurrying off from the

celebrations, and what do I find..." He drawled, leaning against the stone wall. "But my dearest, swooning over a young maiden in the dark corridors."

"I was not swooning," he muttered, a slight scowl touching his dark brow. While he had always been free—even encouraged—to do as he pleased, Tommaso did not like the thought of Alkaios being aware of any special interest he might hold towards a human. His companion had a tendency of finding the smallest things to suddenly become agitated over, which would then awaken his possessiveness of Tommaso.

Sensing his unease, Alkaios reached out to cup the side of his head, smoothing his thumb over his creased brows. "Don't fret so, Maso, it's unbecoming. But do be careful of what trinkets you choose to chase. A nobleman's daughter is a far more noticeable target than that of a farmer's unwanted git."

Tommaso remained silent, but accepted the press of Alkaios' lips to his own, the other man's fingers still threaded through his hair. When they parted he watched his mentor push away from the wall and head back towards the celebrations.

"Come along, I've a few tasty morsels I wish to introduce to you before the night grows too late."

The stars above still shone brightly, but in the distance, there was a faint hint of a softening sky. Dawn would be here soon enough, and he would need to retreat into the darkness of the palace. While the night still allowed it, Tommaso was going to enjoy the openness of the early morning sky, and escape the cage that was this immortal life. He drew a deep breath into his lungs, simply to feel the cool freshness fill him and then released it unused and unneeded.

To his back lay the chambers designated to Alkaios, where their evening's true debauchery had taken place. Bodies of chambermaids and page boys lay strewn over every piece of furniture, dangling as if lifeless. They were not, all had been left with enough blood in their veins to leave them feeling well and truly hungover in the morning—evidence of nothing more than a heavy night of drinking and fornication.

Still, there was a heavy scent of blood in the air, full and completely sated, and it sickened him. His hands pressed to the stone railing of the balcony as he leaned his weight upon it, distancing himself from the room behind. Feeling the cool morning air tickling at his hair, Tommaso closed his eyes and allowed himself to simply be.

Resting in the moment, cold blue eyes returned to his mind, followed by a pale face framed with dark hair. Manette. Her name echoed like a siren's call within his mind and he wondered what this feeling of longing inside of him truly meant. While he had long ago cast aside his vow of chastity, none of his lovers had ever intrigued him in quite this way, not even Alkaios which was born out of something darker. She had spoken barely any words, and what she had uttered were words of disdain—yet the memory of her voice washed over him, leaving his body humming with expectation.

For a moment, Tommaso believed his memory had become so all-encompassing that he was hearing her voice on the winds, only to realize that it was not his imagination, but reality. Peering over the rail and down into the dark gardens below, he made out the slender figures of two women walking quickly over the grass.

"M'lady, please…You should not be out of your chambers at this hour, and without a chaperone!" called the woman hurrying after her, skirts drawn up so she did not trip in her haste.

"I have you," Manette returned crisply, continuing her walk through the garden until she ended up in a dead end, closed in by rose bushes. "And I cannot remain inside *there*, I feel trapped. Encased in stone just as my future is encased in joyless marriage."

As their steps took them further from the palace, Tommaso strained to hear each word carried up to him on the remnants of last eve's winds. The servant, frantic to usher her mistress back beyond the confines of the palace, hurried to her side, only to be brushed off as Manette dropped down onto a stone bench.

"I cannot do what he asks of me Anais, the mere sight of that man repulses me." Manette appeared distraught, burying her face in her hands once the words were torn from her throat. Even from the balcony, Tommaso was able to hear the pain lacing each syllable.

There was a strange urge within himself to go down into those gardens and offer his services in whatever capacity they may be needed. However, his form remained still, even as his mind raced.

"Have you spoken to your father?" the maid questioned, taking a seat on the bench beside the young woman. Gently, she brushed a hand up and down her back.

"A hundred times," Manette dropped her hands into her lap so that teardrop-filled eyes could ponder the woman beside her, as if searching for the answers to life's questions within the lines of her face. "Until my throat has burned in agony and been run raw, but he will not hear it. You know whatever dowry I once had to my name has long been spent by my father…It would seem that Lord Auguste would see us wed without a silver piece to my name. Father wants nothing more than to be rid of me."

Their voices then fell too soft for Tommaso to make out what was being said, no matter how hard he strained. A sudden hand upon his shoulder startled him and he spun to face Alkaios, in all his naked glory, hair mussed and features relaxed.

"Dearest, what draws your attention so entirely that you fail to notice the rising of the morning sun?"

Tommaso shook the thoughts from his head and offered a gentle smile to his companion. "I suppose only the beauty of the early morning. One does miss the way daylight changes their

surroundings." Alkaios laughed softly at these words, slipping an arm around his waist to begin

drawing him into the sanctuary of his chambers. Tommaso followed, as he had always followed these past centuries.

"Sometimes I forget how young you still are, my beautiful fledgling," Alkaios murmured, laughter in his tone. He peered briefly over his shoulder and down into the garden as he ushered Tommaso through the doorway.

6

It would be two evenings before he found occasion to speak to the young maiden once again. When he did, he stumbled upon her in the gardens, hiding away from the demons she faced inside the great hall of King Philip. Unlike before, when the slovenly drunkard had forced her away, Tommaso meant to use this solitude as a means of keeping her speaking until she had decided to do so of her own free will. She had plagued his thoughts since that initial night, and he found himself waking each evening with the sound of her voice ringing in his ears, knowing he had been hearing her within his dreams.

Manette sat not upon the stone bench in the centre of the rose garden, but upon the ground against a bush. Its thorns picked at her royal blue garments and snagged at the strands of her long hair. In her limp hand which lay in the grass beside her, rested a mostly empty bottle of wine from the king's stores. The young woman, it would appear, had drunken herself into quite the daze.

"A lush of a woman was not what I expected to encounter amongst the roses…However, I do not find myself in complaint," he announced with a leisurely drawl as he came upon her.

He found himself impressed with how quickly she glanced up with death in her eyes, to glare at him and respond.

"While you may not find complaint in this situation, I find myself nothing, if not filled with it. Please leave me be…"

There was a true depth of sadness in her plea that had Tommaso pause in his actions and take stock of the situation. While he had no desire to leave her side, he was realizing that if he wished to stay, there was a need to change his current strategy. Moving more cautiously towards her, keeping himself poised in case she attempted to flee, he came to stand before her, slowly lowering himself down to the ground. He kept a respectful distance between them so as not to encroach upon her person too much, but remained close enough to gently pry the wine bottle from her hands.

Bringing it to his own mouth, he sipped from what remained, his eyes staying upon her. Manette watched him through partially lidded eyes, but did not make a move to leave. When he was finished sipping for the mere sake of sipping, Tommaso set the bottle down on the grass between them, and took a moment to truly look upon her face. Manette was beautiful, like the first warm day in early spring, just as the sun rises over the mountains to graze the crystalline depths of a thawing pond. Yet, there was a fragility in her eyes, just like the thin ice upon its surface.

"I know why it is you drink," he announced.

"Oh, please do tell me why." There was scorn in her eyes that melded with the disdain in her tone.

"You are to be married to a boorish slob who is three times your age, and does not hesitate to fondle the servants in your very presence." The thought of this beautiful flower in the paws of that glutton was enough to make even he wish he were able to get drunk.

Manette stared at him for a moment, and then broke into a peel of laughter that both surprised and confused him.

Wiping her eyes with the tips of her fingers, the girl settled back against the bush despite the thorns pricking her flesh. "That was not Lord Auguste, the night you attempted to woo me into your bed, that was my father."

Tommaso felt his brows purse.

"Oh, it was not—"

"No. Lord Auguste, though many years my senior, is actually a handsome man, one which a girl such as myself should be quite happy, and honoured, to wed if she were not to be the next wife in a long line of wives who've all died under strange circumstances. Nor marrying a man who is unable to treat even his own dog with a sliver of respect." This time her laughter was bitter.

"Do you accuse him of the death of his wives?" Tommaso asked, watching her closely in the moonlight.

Manette merely looked back at him, her eyes speaking for her.

"I can help you," Tommaso found himself saying, though he knew not why.

This was exactly the sort of situation Alkaios was continually telling him to refrain from getting involved with. Human lives were so fleeting, gone in the blink of an eye when compared to the never-ending lifespan ahead of him. Yet, he could not seem to stop himself.

"Do not patronize me," Manette spat out, rising quickly to her feet, tugging her skirts free of the thorns before she was able to move away from him.

Not wishing to lose her once more, Tommaso rose without effort to his feet—barring her way in the space of a heart beat.

"I do not patronize, I speak the truth. Let me help you."

"And how are you, a stranger, meant to help me?" Her hand lifted to press to his chest, seeking to move him from her way. However, he was a wall that did not budge, and instead, helped to keep her from swaying on her feet.

"However I may." His own hand lifted to rest overtop hers. There was a sweet scent to her blood, a tinge of desolation and wine, a heady mix that made his baser urges wish to puncture the fluttering pulse at her throat and take a sip. Instead, he fought the natural desire he was not trained to resist, only limit.

"I do not require aid, especially not from a man whose name I do not even know."

"Tommaso, and you do require my aid, or you will be wed to a man who you cannot even stomach to look upon," he murmured, recalling her words from the garden that night.

Manette pulled her hand free from beneath his, and held it clasped to her own bosom instead. "I do not need your help," she repeated, and then stepped around him, her long skirts brushing the side of his leg as she went past.

He let her go this time, feeling the resistance within her— she did not wish for him to follow.

He felt restless, having kept his distance from Manette. There was almost a madness in her eyes whenever she beheld him drawing too near, and so he respected her obvious need for him to stay away. Instead, in-between Alkaios' high demands on his attention, he spent the remaining hours of his nights searching for Lord Auguste. In the end, he was not hard to find.

Wealthy, handsome despite his years, and surrounded by his own men-in-arms, Lord Auguste was as unsavoury a character as Manette had made him out to be. On the surface, he was charming and witty, popular amongst the noblemen and knights alike. However, below the surface there lay a dark force that Tommaso was not unfamiliar with, a monster hid just below the skin—waiting to be unleashed.

Manette was not his concern, yet the soft tread of her footsteps down the hall continued to catch his ear, while her soft, steady voice turned his head each time it sounded out. Something Alkaios did not fail to notice. Tommaso knew better than to mettle, but the notion of her slight frame pinned beneath the weight of the slumbering beast within Auguste disgusted him.

Which was how he came to be following the man one evening as he left the banquet hall. Lord Auguste had imbibed quite heavily in drink, and there was an aura of darkness around him that Tommaso recognized. Tonight, someone was falling prey to an act of viciousness, and he would be there to witness—or possibly prevent—it.

Though half lost to his wine, Auguste moved with intent and purpose, knowing precisely where he wanted to end up. Tommaso could smell the scent of hunger upon him, the lust for feminine wiles, and could only assume he was headed to the chambers of his current bedfellow. His Lordship came upon the door and rapped abruptly on it, and Tommaso was unhappy to find Manette on the other side when at last it opened.

She, it appeared, was just as unhappy to see that Auguste was the one knocking, and sought to prevent him from entering—with no success. Tommaso could only grit his teeth and watch, knowing that none of this was truly his concern and, should he interfere, he would only have Alkaios angry and telling him off for the next several nights.

Those worries were pushed from his mind however, when he heard the distinct sound of Manette crying out in pain and fear rise up from within the room. Unable to restrain himself, Tommaso rushed through the door, to be greeted with the sight of Lord Auguste pinning a struggling Manette against the wall. His slobbering mouth was upon her jaw and throat, his hands around her wrists that were pressed to the wall above her head. Manette, in an attempt to free herself, was thrashing her body against his as best she could, but this seemed only to be exciting the drunk lord hellbent on experiencing his betrothed well before the wedding.

Fury coated his vision as Tommaso crossed the room in an instant. Taking a fistful of Auguste's hair in his hand, he wrenched his head back, and essentially peeled his cloying form from off of Manette. She gasped in relief, and grabbed at the wall to keep herself up. Knowing better, but unable to restrain the wrath frothing in his veins, Tommaso snapped out with his teeth elongated and bit fiercely into Auguste's neck.

The male gasped out in pain, fighting against the ironclad hold Tommaso had upon his form. The beast within Tommaso gloried in the fact Auguste would know what it was like to be trapped against his will, just before his death found him. There was no gentleness offered as he drew the blood from his veins in long, harsh drags, gulping down the hot liquid as quickly as he could.

Just as his heart gave one, last, faltering flicker, Tommaso pulled off him and allowed his slack body to drop lifelessly to the floor, the dull thud sounding triumphantly to his ears. It was the sight of Manette, in a small ball of horror upon the floor, staring at him with eyes filled with terror, that snapped Tommaso from his vindicated fog.

"I'm sorry you had to see that. Are you okay?" he asked softly, moving to stoop down at her side.

Manette scooted back along the wall, keeping her eyes transfixed on his face in her attempt to flee. She thought he meant to do the same to her, could see it in the paler of her skin, and hear it in the frantic beating of her heart.

"Get away from me!" she screamed, tripping on her skirts as she made to get up.

But Tommaso was upon her, gripping her shoulders gently —but firmly—and keeping her in place. "I do not mean you harm, I only wanted to protect you from that brute. I promised you my help…"

She was struggling against him as she had Auguste, fighting the hold as a rabbit fought against the snare. "Please don't kill me!" she sobbed, her form shaking beneath his grasp.

"Manette…" he began, but there was too much fear within her mind for him to speak plainly with her, so instead he reached into her mind with his own, and forced her to calm.

When there was a silent blankness in her eyes, he began to speak, influencing her mind as he did so. "I need you to pack a bag of clothes, and your essentials. We are going to leave the palace tonight before anyone finds Auguste, and I will take you to a place where you can be safe," he informed her softly. Manette, still swept up in the power of his glamour, merely nodded her head. "Now go do that, I will be back in but a moment."

When he released her, the girl rose calmly to her feet and began to move about the room. Having the fortitude to cover his tracks a little, Tommaso lifted Auguste from his place on the floor and laid him out on the bed instead. Once the body was taken care of, Tommaso quickly left Manette's chambers to find his own, gathering what few items he felt that he would need.

This was not what he had intended for tonight, or how he had meant his relationship to evolve with Manette. However, things had proceeded in unexpected ways, and he was left with no choice but to respond.

A part of him longed to leave Alkaios a note, recognizing that the older vampyr would perhaps worry, before being filled with rage at his sudden disappearance. But Tommaso wished to leave nothing behind that might suggest where he had gone, and with whom. In his heart of hearts, he knew that in the end, he would find himself at the side of the other man, once again.

Sack in hand, Tommaso returned to Manette and, with her hand in his, he led her out into the night.

9

When it came time to seek shelter before dawn, Tommaso needed to use his tricks upon Manette once more, convincing her body that she desired to sleep the entire day through. Soon, he would have to release her from the trance he had placed upon her mind, but not yet. Not until they were safe beyond the reach of King Philip, and the even longer reach of Alkaios.

That dusk, as he woke from his death-like slumber, Manette was already awake, sitting huddled in the corner of the abandoned barn he had found them, looking truly lost. Her eyes moved to him as he sat up. For a moment neither of them spoke.

"What do you plan to do with me?" Manette whispered, hands resting atop knees that were drawn up near her chest.

"Whatever it is you wish for me to do. I will take you wherever it is you want to go."

"And then?"

"I will leave you set up so that you can begin the life you want, or I will stay… Whatever you desire once we have reached the place we wish to go." Tommaso found a deep stirring within him for her to want him to remain. He wasn't certain what it was, or why this girl had affected him so, only that he wished to remain in her presence for as long as she would allow it.

"Why?"

He took a moment to consider, before responding. "You are a beautiful young woman trapped in a life not of her choice, with a slovenly, gluttonous parent who seeks not your happiness, but his own ease. I know what it is to have the choice taken from you, and do not enjoy witnessing it happen to another."

She was silent for a moment longer. Her deep, blue eyes studied him in a manner that made him feel exposed.

"What are you?" she asked at last.

"Once, I was a man of God. Now, I am a soulless demon that perhaps seeks his salvation in the rescuing of another life."

"So that wasn't a dream?" Her fingertips raised to brush along the side of her throat. "You killed Lord Auguste by…by—"

"Drinking his blood, yes," he finished for her. "That is how I survive." There was something freeing in being so open with another.

Manette was pale, but to her credit, she did not balk at continuing to meet his gaze. There seemed to be another question on her tongue, but this time she appeared to be faltering at speaking it aloud.

"No," he murmured softly. "I will not feed from you."

She nodded, her eyes falling to the straw-riddled floor. "Where will we go?"

His blood rushed with those four simple words. Whether

she saw no other way out, or had merely resigned herself to his company, for now they would be together.

"Wherever we desire."

Travelling with a human was much slower than Tommaso had remembered. Unable to travel using his own unnatural speed, there was a need instead to locate transportation either by cart or boat. In the end, he found a carriage for hire, and two men willing to take them to the coast, and able to provide nearly round the clock service by switching off between each other.

Manette, it seemed, had decided it best not to question their need of remaining out of the daylight, and instead settled into a quiet state of contemplation as they fled the capital. Knowing the internal struggle when such large changes were sprung upon a person's life, Tommaso did not pry, but left her to her silent reflections.

When Alkaios would begin looking for them, Tommaso could not be certain. All that he could hope was that the elder vampyr would not expect them to be heading to the coast as he had warned Tommaso against travelling by sea if it could be avoided. Too much time spent confined on the water and one would run out of viable veins to sup from without causing obvious death and disease. So, in hopes of leading him astray, that was exactly what Tommaso planned to do. While the passage across the waters into the kingdom of England was not a long one, he hoped it would be enough to throw Alkaios off their scent. From there, they would settle on a final destination for Manette.

He had begun to think they would pass the entire duration

in silence, but at last Manette found her voice around him once more, and began to speak.

"I've never been to the ocean," she announced one evening, just after they had stopped for both of them to feed and then returned to their closed in carriage to resume. "It was something I always desired to see, but Father saw no value in the time, or coins, spent to do so. If nothing else comes of this, I suppose at least I will have achieved that."

"I am pleased to be the one to help you see it done. The waters of the ocean are vast and turbulent—both beautiful, and deadly." He thought about the last time he had felt the cold spray of ocean water upon his cheek. "I've only seen the sunlight sparkling upon its surface once, when I was a young boy, but the moonlight can cast a breathtaking gleam over its rippling waters also." He glanced across the carriage to Manette, peering into the dark cast of her eyes in the moonlight. "I think the ocean will speak to you."

Like the waters of the ocean, Tommaso was coming to find that Manette's inner strength ran deep. There was an essence to her that could not be contained, and would fight against any attempts at restraining it.

"I hope that it does."

Though conversation did not flow frequently between them, it was no longer an entirely silent trip, and as time wore on, a side of humour and laughter began to show in the young woman steadily blossoming beneath the mantle of freedom.

When at last they came to the coastline, Tommaso pounded the roof to signal their drivers should stop. He helped Manette out of the carriage, and led her across the rocky shore to the narrow strip of sand leading to the water's edge. The breeze coming in off the ocean was cold upon his cheeks, tussling his hair about in its cool fingers and bringing with it the scent of salt and seaweed.

"Oh…" It was a whispered word of amazement that slipped passed Manette's lips as she stared out over the vastness of the water. "It is never ending."

He felt a little smile tug at his lips. "Yes, it does appear that way. Beautiful, isn't it?" he asked, eyes upon her face as she beheld the sight before them.

"Even more so than I had dreamed," was her response, a smile of delight upon her face that filled Tommaso's form with gladness.

Before he could speak another word, Manette was stooping down to slip out of her shoes and stockings, lifting her skirts to wade ankle deep into the water. A soft gasp slipped form her lips as she felt the shock of its chill upon her flesh. Tommaso merely stepped back, and took enjoyment in watching her happiness. He hadn't thought himself to be jaded already, but the many centuries by Alkaios' side, only seeing humans as something to sup, and bed, had stolen form him the appreciation for their tendencies toward wonder and awe.

Dropping her skirts into the water, Manette waded in further, until the cold ocean was up to her knees. She stooped down to scoop up some, bringing it to her lips to take a drink. She had done it before he could warn her against such actions, and he lifted a hand to hide his chuckles of laughter as she spat it back out.

"It really is unbearably full of salt." Even this seemed to delight her, for she cast him a smile over her shoulder.

In that moment, Tommaso felt he could stand there and watch Manette's joy in the ocean until the sun rose in the morning sky and burnt him to ashes.

Having managed to broker their passage on a vessel leaving for England the next evening, Tommaso was relieved there would be no need to smuggle him aboard, hidden from the sunshine inside a wooden trunk. Instead, he tucked himself away in an inn nearby, and suggested Manette spend what time by the sun-drenched sea shore she could.

Though he had mostly removed his glamour from her mind, he was not concerned with her running away while he slept. Something had settled in Manette during their carriage ride to the coast and, once they had arrived at the waters, a new sense of freedom had filled her. Tommaso could see it there within her eyes—Manette was beginning to believe there was hope of a new life for her.

Soon enough they were sequestered inside the belly of the ship, a dank space tucked away in the bow, just enough room for them to stow their trunks and tuck themselves into the swaying hammocks. It did not bother Tommaso. In some ways, the cradling netting rocking him to and fro on each new swell of the ocean brought back faint memories of his childhood, and a mother who used to sing him to sleep.

"Your eyes grow dim," Manette murmured later that evening as they stood on the deck of the ship. He had thought they were both gazing out over the waters, but it would seem her attention had been elsewhere. "Are you ill? Can you… grow ill?"

"I am quite all right," he assured her. "I simply did not feed to the extent I needed before we set sail, and I dare not try my hand at one of the crew lest I be caught."

It did mean that being below deck, confined to such a tight

space with the sweetness of Manette's scent surrounding him, was almost unbearable. He had stomached the carriage ride due to his ability to find fresh veins at each resting point they took. Even still, most mornings he had met his slumber with the prick of sharp incisors against his bottom lip—in many ways, she was his delight and also his torment.

"I could…give you some, if you need it?"

"No," he responded more sharply than he intended. Shaking his head, Tommaso reached over to gently place his hand upon hers. "While I am touched by such an offer, I will not feed on you." For fear he would not be able to stop himself, or the pleasure of her taste would ignite a desire for another pleasure to be met, and he would simply take things too far.

While every part of him wished to devour Manette, to experience her to the last drop until he was branded upon every inch of her being, Tommaso knew for certain that he would never allow himself to—not until the day she specifically asked for it.

"If you are certain," came her soft reply. Blue eyes dark in the moonlight studied him closely.

"I am."

They came upon England some twenty hours after leaving shore, the sun having just set and provided Tommaso with the cover that he needed. Disembarking, Tommaso felt himself grow lighter as their feet touched down upon soil once again. With such a large body of water between them, he felt that perhaps at last, he and Manette could cease looking over their shoulders.

8

"Are you certain?" Manette crushed the soft fabric of the gown to her chest as she admired herself in the mirror, while Tommaso looked on in pleasure.

For five days they had been safely tucked away in the fortified town of Warick. In this time Tommaso had won the favour of the influential earl, Lord Thomas, and earned a place for the both of them in his beautiful stone castle. While it wasn't precisely the lap of luxury that residing within a king's palace afforded them, it was enough to provide them with daily entertainment, and a proper bed beneath them. It was also giving them the opportunity to attend a ball Lord Thomas was throwing in celebration of the nuptials of his eldest son.

"Of course I am. You had naught with you that would suffice for such an evening, and it brings me pleasure to see you thus. We came away so that you might enjoy life, and tonight at the ball you shall do just that, new gown and all."

It wasn't as refined a gown as the ones found at court, but

for the earl of Warwick's estate, it would more than just do. Manette would shine amidst the other guests, her natural beauty and youth a beacon for all wandering in the darkness of age.

"Thank you so very much, Maso… I look forward to a night of dining and music where I am not being paraded out like a prized sheep to the highest bidder, but simply there to enjoy the evening."

It pleased him to hear her say such things, for when Manette was happy, Tommaso found that he was as well. The smile curving her lips in this moment was enough to make his own blood sing.

"Then if you are ready, let us go." He offered his hand to her, feeling her accept it without hesitation.

Free of her father's shadow she had blossomed, and with it, had come a new ease between them. A friendship of sorts that brought him more deeply into her confidence. Tommaso had forgotten what it was like to know a person's heart and mind rather than the dips and curves of their body, to be allowed into their innermost thoughts and cares. She was causing him to realize he had spent centuries feasting upon the shallow treats of life that held no substance, and now he was being returned to the true fruit of life.

Leading her down the long hallway of the estate, towards the long sweeping staircase that would take them into the main area of the home, Tommaso felt his chin rise with pride. He had done precisely what he had told her he would do— free her from an uncaring father who wished to marry her off to a man of violence. And in doing so, had freed himself from a presence he had not fully realized was becoming stifling to himself.

Alkaios was the one who had taken him in when he had nothing, and knew nothing of himself, or the ways of the vampyr. While he would always have a love in his heart for the life they had built together, an eternity was too long to live at the behest of someone else. Perhaps now he could live a life of freedoms that were meant solely for himself, and fulfilling his desires. Manette just so happened to be his first step towards this.

Their steps carried them quickly towards the large ball-room that took up a large portion of the manor's east side. Large columns supported the ceiling above, and a series of long wooden tables ran down the sides of the room, heavy-laden with food. Already, music was being played as couples mulled about, making introductions and reacquainting them-selves with old companions. The newly married couple sat in a place of honour at the head of the room, sipping from goblets of wine and teasingly feeding each other bites of food from their fingertips.

"I believe they are about to start the first dance. May I have the honour, or is your card already filled?" he jested.

"I would be delighted to accept." She smiled up at him as she removed her hand from his arm to place it in his own hand instead, allowing him to lead her out.

Taking their positions across from each other, they easily fell into the steps as music swelled around them. Tommaso blocked out the soft chatter of guests and concentrated instead on the brightness of Manette's eyes, and the touch of her hand as they met together, spinning and dipping before stepping apart once more. The movements, though innocent enough in nature, were igniting within him a hunger that made his dark brown eyes dilate, and his teeth sharpen. Now was not the time to find himself drawn to the column of her throat, but it was happening anyway.

As the dance came to a close, Tommaso led her straightway into another, finding himself unwilling to release her into the room at large. In this moment, her eyes were upon him, as was her full attention, and it was exactly where he wanted them to be. Releasing her hand so that they could dance around the outside of the line of couples, only to reunite at the other end, Tommaso watched her over the heads of the other maidens. Though there was beauty all around him, she was the only one he truly desired. Manette was the target of his need, the scent that stirred him, and the only one he could not allow himself to have—yet.

As the second dance concluded, he offered a breathless Manette his arm, pressing his free hand down overtop hers. "Let's get you some refreshments." Together they moved into the buffet line, picking from the delicious offerings.

While Manette made her choices, Tommaso plucked glasses of wine from a passing servant's tray, and carried them down the line until at last they were ready to find a seat. It was as they were taking their places that another scent caught his attention, sparking his own thirst. Peering around, he found its origin—a pretty footman who did not look away as their eyes met.

"If you would not find it altogether rude… I would excuse myself to feed as well," he questioned, eyes falling to read her expression.

While she did not like it, Manette had grown used to his needs and ways, and did not hold him back when he declared it time to sate them. "Of course. I will be here still when you return."

Plucking her hand up, he kissed the top of it, meeting her eyes for a moment, and then turned. Making his way to the young footman, he requested softly in his ear that he lead him to a quiet place in the gardens where he could partake in some fresh air.

Not understanding fully what was about to happen, but realizing there was something in the air between them, the lad ushered him to a set of large doors. It took them out onto a stone balcony with the offering of steps leading into the gardens below. Outside, Tommaso murmured for the footman to follow him, and together they descended into the darkness provided by the cool evening.

When they were free of potential observation, Tommaso drew the lad towards him, his hand lifting to cup his cheek as he brushed a thumb over his lips. Unable to resist the pliant nature of the lovely creature before him, Tommaso dipped his head to kiss him, tasting the youthful essence of his life. He contemplated pressing him against one of the nearby trees and sating another growing hunger, instead he broke from his lips and pressed his chin lightly so as to expose the pale line of his throat.

"You are a beautiful, willing treat," he murmured, then lowered his lips to the pulse beating there beneath the surface of silken flesh, and sunk his teeth into him. The male released a soft whimper of pain, his hands coming to clutch at Tommaso's chest in an effort to push him away, yet he did not cry out for help.

The taste of fear coated his tongue, and the subtle feel of a struggle within his grasp ignited the ravenous, clawing beast inside of him that was never sated. He could have, and likely should have, swayed the boy's mind into clouded submission, but the darkest parts of himself needed to feed upon the desperation of another, to feel the fragile life of his prey grasping at living. It was a part of himself that would never die, a part that Alkaios had insisted he accept and indulge when the situation presented itself.

He had meant to only sip from him, to take just enough to get him through the evening and perhaps the next without requiring more blood, but there was something in the growing struggle as the young footman felt his life draining from him that caused Tommaso to press on.

He drank deeply of the life-giving liquid that now flowed so freely from his companion. Strong hands now pushed with more force, as a new found fear coursed through what remained within him.

It should have had Tommaso releasing him, but he had now been so many days denying his true nature that the impulse was too hard to suppress any longer. He wrapped one arm around the other male's more slender frame, pinning his arms to his sides, and crushing his chest into his own. As the last bout of fight filled the boy, Tommaso released a growl of pleasure against his flesh and gulped down blood in a gluttonous manner until the form against his own grew slack. He felt his heartbeat growing weak and eventually cease altogether.

Pulling off him with a gasp, Tommaso gazed down at the blank face and dim eyes staring lifelessly up at the star-filled night, cursing himself and his own weakness. There had been no cause for death tonight, beyond selfish cravings. His own body now alive with the thrill of hunting, feeding and then killing, he bent to scoop the lifeless one easily into his arms. Carrying him deeper into the gardens, he found a secluded place where he quickly dug a hole and buried the young man within it.

"I thank you for your sacrifice," he whispered apologetically to him, before closing his eyes and, lastly, covering his face with soil.

Filled with not nearly enough regret, Tommaso made his way back into the castle, bright with lights and music, searching for Manette amid the throng. In her happy smile he found redemption, and put the dead footman far from his thoughts.

9

London, England

Manette sat across from him, a glass of wine in her hand, and laughter upon her lips, as she spoke candidly with another young woman she had made friends with shortly after their arrival in London three weeks earlier. It pleased Tommaso immensely to see the way she continued to blossom in her new life, finding more ways to enjoy the freedom that was now hers. Being here in the city brought them a little closer to France, but also nearer the aristocrats, providing him with ample fodder to work with, so that finding a home for the two of them had been no trouble at all.

In the end, they had decided to portray themselves as husband and wife, avoiding questions of them living together when they were unattached. This lie, of course afforded them more opportunities to be close and ever-so personal with each other, which in turn was making them closer in actuality. Each time Tommaso stepped out with Manette on his arm, he prided himself in having won her over that evening in Paris, convincing her to trust him enough to whisk her away from a life she detested.

"You must come to the tourney being held in a fortnight! Watching all those knights duelling in armour and seeing which of the maidens offers up her favour… It's all delightfully scandalous," Miriam was chattering on, and as she spoke, Manette's eyes drifted to his across the room.

"That sounds splendid my dear," he agreed. "I'll be away on business at that time, so you should join Miss Stewart at the tournament so that my absence is not so hard on you."

He could not deny her a life in the sunlight when she was human, and born to it. Plus, should neither of them ever show up in daylight hours, people would begin to talk, and Tommaso would rather not have to glamour all of them into forgetting their suspicions. His response elicited a bright smile from Manette, and she nodded quickly to Miriam.

"Then it is settled!" Miriam chimed. "I'll send round our carriage for you first thing in the morning on the twentieth."

Manette had returned home flushed and happy, her blue eyes glowing with a warmth that he never wished to deny her. If her being able to go out into the world and enjoy life to the fullest without him was what it would take to keep her happy, then he would provide her with every opportunity to do so.

Tommaso joined her for her evening meal shortly after he woke, allowing her to talk endlessly about what she had experienced—the bravery as well as stupidity, of the knights as they competed for glory and monetary reward. Sipping his glass of blood, Tommaso chuckled when appropriate, and questioned her further on her activities, simply taking his own pleasure in seeing her so happy. It was intoxicating, almost as much as the fresh blood passing between his lips, knowing that he had helped give her this.

Eventually they settled in the sitting room. Situated near the fire, they began to speak of more personal things.

"I've never asked you… when… how did it happen?" Manette eyed him with tenderness, and while it was not a topic he enjoyed speaking about, he could see her need to know and understand.

"It was a very, very long time ago," he began. "In the monastery on Monte Cassino, in Italy."

"Monastery?" Her eyes widened in surprise, and she studied him more closely.

Tommaso offered an amused smile, knowing her thoughts. "Yes, I was dedicated to the abbey when I was fifteen, the middle son of my parents. It had always been allotted for me, and I was happy in it." He felt a wistfulness settle over him as he thought of memories he hadn't allowed himself to in a very long time. "However, one night a dark creature attacked one of the young brothers, and in my attempt to save him, I, too, was attacked. I woke up the next evening alone in a cave, and I was forever transformed."

"You were alone?" There was a deep frown upon her features which, though unpleasant considering her previous happiness, touched him nonetheless.

"I was… and for many years to follow. Until an older vampyr took pity upon me, and took me into his home teaching me our ways."

"The Greek man who was there with you…?"

"Alkaios." He nodded. "Yes, it was him."

"Oh," she whispered, the word holding so much more than its soft exhalation would typically imply. "Does it sadden you? To have left him because of me?"

Tommaso shook his head gently, offering a subtle smile. "No, not at all. Alkaios and I had many, many years together, and now it is my time to be on my own, and find for myself who I truly am."

His words eased something within her, for Manette's shoulders relaxed. "Something we have in common it would seem."

Manette was suddenly upon her feet. Crossing the room, she offered her hand to him. Questioningly, Tommaso took the tiny hand, and allowed himself to be drawn up to his feet. Looking down at her, he was surprised to find she did not step back, but instead, stepped nearer.

"Maso, you are the best man that I have ever known." Her words were soft as her hands came to rest upon his chest. "That is who you are."

He could hear her heart tripping along at a faster pace, and without hesitation lowered his head to kiss her lips. A part of himself expected Manette to draw back, instead she melted into him, a soft sigh of pleasure leaving her. Feeling her happy response, Tommaso lifted his hands to cup her face, tipping her head back enough that he could deepen the kiss with a gentle intrusion. Instinctively her lips parted to him and he felt a faint moan leave him.

This was what he had desired from the moment their eyes had met across the room in King Philip's palace, but which he had not allowed himself to believe he would receive. As her form molded easily into his own, Tommaso stooped a little so that he could lift her light frame into his arms. Their lips did not part as he made the ascent to her chambers, closing the door behind them with his foot.

In her room, he set her carefully back on her feet, pulling away at last so he could look down into her eyes, searching for fear or refusal. Instead, he found only eager consent. With deft fingers, Tommaso began to undo the stays of her dress, loosening the fabric until it was free enough to slip down over her body. Just the sight of her in the thin shift had his own blood coursing more hurriedly.

Their mouths sought each other out once more in a needy, hungry connection, both their hands working on removing his own clothing. Once they were in nothing but her shift and his breeches, Tommaso captured her by the backs of her thighs, lifting her up to then stretch her out on the bed. Hovering over her, his lips brushed reverent kisses down her neck and over her shoulders, hands tugging at the hem of her shift to tug it up over her hips, so his fingers could explore the soft, warm flesh that readily welcomed him there.

Manette gasped in pleasure at each new sensation. Tommaso took his time to kiss and nip over each new exposed curve of flesh, delighting in her little moans and surprised whimpers. When at last their bodies came together, he gazed down into her eyes, feeling the connection that lay there beyond the surface, tying the two of them together in a way their bodies never could.

Afterwards, laying with limbs entwined, and her body slowly cooling, Manette ran her fingers lovingly through his hair.

"How is it you have such a wonderful head of hair when your life was frozen at a point when you would have had it shaven?"

Her curiosity caused him to chuckle happily, and Tommaso tightened his arms around her, drawing her nearer.

"Each day my body heals itself, restoring anything that has been injured or removed. So my hair continues to grow as a natural regeneration of my form," he explained, amusement in his dark eyes.

"Fascinating," Manette whispered, and her simple contentment in that answer was enough to bring his lips to hers once more, tasting the sweetness that was there.

Life had fallen into such a simple rhythm of happiness, Tommaso should have known it was never meant to last. It began as a meeting of familiar faces, friends made during their stay those first few weeks in the countryside. Seeking to make a life for themselves that was as normal as could be, Tommaso had agreed to the couple joining them for an evening meal at their home.

The meal passed in pleasant conversation, the four of them enjoying each other's company. Finished speaking of the excitement that had been had in London as of late, Manette questioned them on Lord Thomas and his household, and Sarah was all to pleased to fill them in on the gossip there was to share.

"Oh! You missed all the scandal that came about just after you left," Sarah stated, leaning in a little so that she could meet Manette's eyes directly. "One of Lord Thomas' footmen disappeared," she announced. "They thought perhaps he had run off with one of the village girls."

"Would have been better for the lad if he had," Jonathon quipped.

Tommaso felt himself stiffen as the conversation turned to an area that felt a little too close for comfort.

"Well, the young will be young…" he said casually, his eyes not daring to look down the table to Manette.

"But he hadn't run off!" Sarah declared.

"No? What happened?" Manette questioned, curious.

"Well, one of Thomas' hounds dug his body up in the gardens! Someone had buried him beneath the rose bushes!" Sarah had the decency to look scandalized, even though her eyes shone with the excitement of it all.

"No…" Manette responded. Her voice soft and troubled, drew Tommaso's eye.

"Yes, and that isn't even the worst of it," Jonathon stated, before sipping from his wine. "Something had bit his throat, he had a terrible gash there. What sort of person bites someone else?"

Manette's eyes lifted across the table and caught his, the troubled light within them growing. There was a question for him in their depths, one which he did not want to answer. He could simply tell her it was not him, or glamour her questions away, but they were at such a point now he wasn't certain he could bring himself to do it.

The atmosphere was tense after that, and while they both behaved as gracious hosts, Tommaso knew the questions that were sure to come. No sooner had the door closed on Sarah and Jonathon, but Manette was turning on him, a desperate look on her face.

"Please tell me that was not you," she rasped in a soft voice, begging him to tell her that her suspicions were wrong.

"Please tell me you did not kill that boy when you have no need of it, when I know you have no need of it!"

He should have told her no, there was always the possibility that she would have believed him. Instead, he told her the truth.

"Yes," he whispered. "I didn't intend to... but I simply lost control." Which wasn't entirely true, he had simply wanted to kill. Had needed to kill, to fill that void inside of him that was only silenced with the death of another at his hands.

"You're a monster." It came out harshly, forced past a sob that was working at strangling her words.

"Manette, darling..." He stepped forward, reaching for her hand, only to have her pull it back out of his grasp.

"Don't touch me! To think that I have let you touch me!" She shook her head, disgust upon her features.

"You've seen me kill before..."

"That was different! He was a horrid man who was hurting me, not a young servant only doing what you asked!" Tears were springing to her eyes, and he made another move toward her, but this time she stepped back, her head shaking. "No."

Manette left then, turning around and leaving directly out the front door. She took nothing with her, not even a shawl as she slipped into the darkness beyond. He wanted to stop her, but there was a finality as the door closed, and he was left standing alone in the house that had just hours before, been filled with such happiness.

10

She had not returned by the time the sun began to brighten the sky. Wanting to go and look for her, Tommaso was forced to retreat into his blacked out chambers, and be consumed by his day slumber. When he woke with a gasp that night, it was to find Manette still not home, and a newfound worry began to fill him. What if something had happened to her? He should have followed her into the night, rather than let her go.

Not taking the time to feed, Tommaso grabbed Manette's shawl and headed for the front door. He would track her down if it were the last thing he did. Perhaps she had gone to Miriam's and was simply avoiding him…

He never made it to the door. A voice called to him from the darkness of the sitting room, and brought him to an abrupt halt. A shiver of dread coursed through him as, slowly he turned to stare at the male seated casually in the tall armchair.

"Alkaios…"

"Darling, did you think you would be allowed to leave me without so much as a word?"

"I thought perhaps you were too busy to care," he responded slowly, trying to keep his eyes on Alkaios while he also kept an ear open for the chance of anyone else in the house with them.

The other man hissed in displeasure. "You know very well that is not true, nor was it ever." He stood, straightening the jacket over his frame.

In the blink of an eye, Alkaios was suddenly before him, a hand to his throat and thrusting him back against the wall, pinning him there. With a grunt he hit the door frame with his elbow and the wood splintered beneath the action.

Green eyes nearly glowed with anger as Alkaios leaned in close enough that his breath fanned out over Tommaso's lips. "I dedicated hundreds of years to you, showing you this world, and all that is open to us in it, and how do you repay me and my love?"

His words were a growl, and his hand tightened around Tommaso's throat. Had he need of air, he would have been gasping for it. Instead, he only winced at the tightness, and feared the possibility Alkaios may tear his head clean from his shoulders.

"I wanted something new," he rasped brokenly.

"New," Alkaios spat the word out. "I gave you new every night. You wanted that girl, and you threw away our lives for it." He pulled Tommaso away from the wall only to thrust him back against it, causing his form to indent it.

Tommaso would have fought, but there was no point. Alkaios was ancient compared to him, and his strength far surpassed his own. All he could do was hope that once he was tired of raving over his upset, he would release him.

"Yes, I did." There was no sense in denying it. "And I would do it all over again, just for a chance at the happiness she and I had."

A real sense of connection that had never been there during all his years of following along wherever Alkaios dragged him.

With a growl of discontent, the other vampyr lashed out at him, releasing his throat, but only so that his teeth could sink into it instead. Tommaso cried out at the searing pain of his mentor viciously gulping down his blood, drawing from him what was never meant to be taken. Struggling against him now, feeling the much-needed life leaving his undead form, he did what he could to fight him off.

In the end it was futile, as he had known it would be, and Tommaso sunk into the darkness.

He regained consciousness to the scent of musty, dank water, and stale air. Groaning, he slowly sat up, feeling weak in a way he had not felt in many centuries, and a thirst for blood that was so intense he could not retract his fangs. Looking around him, Tommaso realized that he was in a dungeon of sorts. Alkaios hadn't gotten him into the actual palace had he?

While the bars tauntingly offered a means of escape, the sluggish feel of his body gave him all the answer he could want. There would be no escaping this cell until Alkaios saw fit to release him.

"So you've woken."

Tommaso looked through the darkness of the dungeon to find Alkaios in the shadows, his form swathed in black. He hissed unhappily at the sight of him, shifting on the slab of stone that was his bed, and leaning back against the damp wall.

"Where do you have me?" he demanded.

"The where is not important, but the why," Alkaios responded, slowly moving towards the cell.

Tommaso waited, and when he didn't continue he rolled his eyes. "Then, why?"

Alkaios reached out to grip the bar before him, squeezing it lightly as he leaned in towards Tommaso's cell. His handsome features calm even in his madness, chin length hair loose and falling around his cheeks.

"Retribution. You took from me what I valued most, and now I do the same to you."

"My freedom?"

Alkaios only smiled, a smile that did not reach his eyes, and sent a chill of concern racing through him. This question was not answered. His former companion merely continued to watch him until, at last, he pulled away from the bars.

"Enjoy your time down here, you've plenty of it. I would suggest using it wisely and truly contemplating what you should have done differently." The older vampire then turned and began to walk away. "Try not to get too hungry," he murmured with a dark chuckle, then disappeared up a set of stone stairs.

Tommaso watched him go, then settled back to wait out his punishment, whatever Alkaios had settled on as a long enough time for him to make his point. Tommaso believed that he would make do without feeding easily enough for quite a while, however, he had never been drained of most of his blood before and then left with no chance to recuperate.The hunger came upon him in a matter of days, so vast and all-encompassing that he felt the edges of his mind warping.

In a need to feel his teeth biting down into flesh, he bit into his own wrist, lapping at what remained of the blood in his veins, though it lacked the life-giving essence of human blood. It wasn't enough, or even a touch of what he truly needed, and it was becoming more than what he could bear. Not even his day-slumber was enough to help, and his thirst heightened to such an extent that even the true sleep was denied him.

When he heard the door at the top of the stairs finally open, he felt an immense sense of relief. Finally, he would be released. Finally, he would have a chance to feed and quench this agonizing need inside of him. Alkaios was not alone—the wonderful scent of fresh, human blood made its way down to him, and his fangs throbbed in response as his body nearly spasmed.

Tommaso was on his feet and racing to the cage as quickly as his weakened body would allow him. Face pressed into the bars, he fought the urge to beg for whoever it was that Alkaios had brought to him.

When they came into view though, Tommaso shrunk back, pressing his body against the wall to try and contain himself. The young woman with an open gash on her wrist was Manette, and her eyes showed no sense of relief at the sight of him, rather anger and resentment more deeply settled within them than ever before.

His own chest began to rise and fall quickly, much like a wild animal being cornered. The scent of her blood on the air was enough to drive the beast within him crazy, and he knew that it would take every ounce of what little strength remained not to try and pull her through the bars.

"What? Are you not pleased to see your little plaything,

my pet?" Alkaios asked, a smirk of satisfaction gleaming in his eyes. "I've only been looking after her for you, and such an insolent pet she is." He made a tsking noise, as if Manette could be held accountable for anything she had done while under his detainment.

"Manette, has he hurt you?" Tommaso looked at her as he spoke, his eyes travelling over her form in concern.

"I'm fine," was her clipped response. "Or as well as one may be after they've been tricked by a monster, and then held captive by his owner."

The words struck him harshly to the chest, for the truth of them was there, and easy to see. Tommaso had lost himself to his banal instincts and allowed the life Alkaios lived to take him over, never once questioning what it was they were doing.

"I am so very sorry, Manette," he whispered.

She gave no answer, but Alkaios chuckled, shaking his head. "Oh, to have been witness to this lovers quarrel, it is truly a delight. Now… why don't we reunite you properly and see if we can't settle things between you, once and for all?"

Upon hearing his words, Tommaso roared in protest, pressing himself back against the wall even more. Wishing, in fact, to disappear into it. He knew what would happen should she be set inside the cell with him.

"Alkaios, please! I beg of you!"

The turning of a metal key inside the latch was his only response, and as the cell door squeaked open, he pressed his hands to his face, hoping to block out the world. He kept them there, even after the cell door clanged shut once more, and Manette was firmly locked within. Tommaso fought to keep his mind blank and his senses off, but the predator in him knew full well there was a delectable feast now within arms reach, and it had been so very long.

Lifting his head, he peered over at her, fangs denting his bottom lip and a low growl slipping from somewhere deep in his throat. She was paler than she had been, her own chest rising and falling with each fearful gasp—she knew, knew that he was no longer within his right mind.

Tommaso was taken back to those first days of his change, when the hunger was upon him and he had taken the lives of those he loved and respected. He had fought to control that beast, to keep it contained, but there was no caging a wild creature who was starving.

"Are you going to kill me?" she whispered, unshed tears in her eyes.

He wanted to reassure her that he would never harm her, that since the moment he had first laid eyes upon her he had loved her for her beauty, her grace, and for the underlying strength in everything she did. But with each rapid beat of her terrified heart, the scent of her fresh-flowing blood spread further through the room. It was in his nostrils and upon his tongue—body trembling, Tommaso shook his head. Perhaps he was trying to convince himself that he could take only a small amount.

It was happening before either of them realized, Tommaso having crossed the room at a wholly unnatural speed, and his arms clasped about her. This embrace was much different from all the ones that had come before, and as his teeth sunk into the column of her neck, he couldn't help but think of their time on the ship. He had vowed never to take from her, never to feed upon her veins, for she was a creature too valuable and dear to his heart.

Now, as the warm, coppery blood flowed freely over his tongue, and her cries of pain and fear echoed in his ears, Tommaso felt his own eyes fill with tears. They welled up, only to fall down his cheeks as he continued to gulp greedily from her, his body demanding everything and all, wanting to leave not a single drop.

When her body began to grow limp, and her cries had reduced to nothing but wasted whimpers, Tommaso managed to pull himself off of her, gasping in despair as he looked down at her drawn features. Cupping her cheek, he slipped fingers lightly beneath her head to draw it up.

"Manette….darling…" he rasped, begging for her eyes to open, to show that she was still alive. When they did so, he shuddered in relief. "I am so sorry…"

He wanted to assure her that it would be all right, that they were both going to be all right, but he could hear the shallowness of her breath and the pitiful way her heart beat. There wasn't enough blood left to sustain her, and soon she would be gone.

"I can save you," he rushed. Lifting his wrist to his mouth he tore at the veins there, bringing the open wound to her mouth. "Drink, please!"

Manette, with her last bout of strength turned her head away, spitting out any drops of blood that had reached her mouth.

"No." Her eyes held a defiant light, even in her weakness. "I will not become one of you. Let me keep my soul and die, rather than lose it and live to be a monster like the both of you."

Tommaso now openly wept, feeling all the sins of his life come rushing back to him. Had his path always been leading him to this moment, to holding the new love of his life in his arms, and watching whatever sense of real fulfillment he may have possessed slowly fade away?

"Please…" he pleaded, trying to bring his wrist to her mouth once more, but the look in her eyes held him still and he let his hand fall. Instead, he drew her into the safe cradle of his arms.

Slowly, Tommaso sank to the floor, allowing her body to ease down over his lap as he rested her head against the crook of his arm. His fingertips brushed lightly over her cheek as he felt her weakening, the ebbing rhythm of her heart descending towards finality.

"I love you," he whispered to her, wanting her to know at least that.

"No," she replied, shaking her head, and with a last breath of denial upon her lips, she died.

II

To say that he lost a part of himself in that dungeon would not be an exaggeration. Something took place in those dark depths that forever changed him. For over six centuries, he had allowed himself to wallow in this sense of pain and loss, thinking only of what fate and that monster in the night had taken from him, not of what he had taken from the world. Tommaso had thought with the loss of his soul and human life that there could be no more left to lose, but Alkaios had made sure to prove him wrong.

When at last the cell door opened, and his once beloved mentor set him free, Tommaso clasped Manette's body close to his chest and carried her past him, heading directly for the stairs.

"Have you no words for me, after all of this time?" Alkaios called after him.

A part of Tommaso wished to tear the other man asunder, to see him in the same amount of agony that he was currently feeling, but to even try would be his death. Another part felt a sort of peace in that thought, of finally seeing an end to it all. Yet, what had his life amounted to, to be fine with ending it now? Nothing of value, not as he had once vowed it would.

147

Instead of attacking him, Tommaso merely paused on the stone steps, not turning to look upon his face for fear he would not be able to contain his fury.

"There is nothing left to say," he rasped, his voice cold and empty. "You have had your retribution, now let this be the end of it. All of it… You, me, and this madness we have been living." He swallowed down further words of contempt that he wished to say, and instead settled on, "Should we ever cross paths again… I will find a way to kill you."

Having said his peace, Tommaso left his mentor to the depths of the dungeon and the untold darkness of his own essence and desires. When he stepped at last into the fresh air of the night, all he could do was hold Manette even closer to his chest. He would give her a proper burial, somewhere lovely and becoming of her.

Perhaps somewhere on a cliff overlooking the water, so she might always taste the salt air upon her tongue.

Lifting his eyes to the heavens, he sought the vastness of its expanse, searching for answers in the stars. As a human Tommaso had lived a life devoted to God and mankind, a life of discipline and love, of selflessness. A humble human life offered up to the service and care of others had brought more happiness than any vampyr Tommaso had felt in all of this eternal debauchery.

What could life give you, if you gave nothing back?

Holding Manette's lifeless form close to his unbeating heart, Tommaso wondered if it was time to find a new life to live, a new version of himself that could find happiness in being more than just death's counterpart. A life of careless greed and senseless death had not helped to cover the feelings of guilt carried deep inside him, and while he could wash the blood off his hands, he could not wash the responsibility of life ended from his being.

Tommaso held Manette in his arms for the length of time it took him to walk to the coast, finding a lone cliff overlooking the ocean where he was able to dig a hole to tenderly place her in. Even in death her beauty was daunting, leaving him filled with a mixture of emotions only she had ever been able to elicit within him. She had longed for nothing more than a happy life lived well and, as the being he currently was, there had been no hope of ever giving it to her.

Slowly, he had covered her body with soft, brown soil, erasing her presence from the world, though never from his memory. Manette would be the last life taken in vain by his hands. That was the new vow he made to himself, and the Creator who had turned his back upon him.

There would be no more death, not by his hands, or by any other that he could prevent. Perhaps there was a way to blend his life of old, and the abilities of his damned existence. To become someone new, someone better.

Perhaps life could offer up something greater, if he only sought to give back to it something better.

Sitting beside Manette's graveside, his eyes lifted once more to the stars, and he took his time counting the glistening lights present in the vast body. Atonement was always found one step at a time, and he had an immortal lifetime ahead of him to seek it out.

Epilogue

1983 CE - New York State

He stood glancing out the window, the sun having just set and cast the world in a soft, comforting darkness, when a knock came at his study door.

"Come in," he called out, slowly turning, hands clasped behind his back.

He was surprised to see two young girls enter, one a human, and one a purebred vampire. The worn looks upon their face informed him that this was not a casual surprise visit, but that these two strangers were in search of something.

"Hello…" he stated casually, a studying look upon his features.

"I'm sorry to just barge in uninvited, but the guy at the front door said it was okay… We heard that you help vampires who need it," the human girl announced, reaching out to take the hand of the other girl beside her. "My name is Erin, and this is my friend Dinah."

"I help vampires who deserve it," he corrected, smiling gently at the young lives. There was a stricken look on Dinah's face, and through her guilt he saw a reflection of himself many, many centuries ago.

Moving around his desk he crossed the room towards the two of them, and extended his hand to Dinah. "It is nice to meet you, Dinah. Please come in, both of you, and tell me how I may help you."

There was a relieved look on both of their faces, and one of happy validation upon Erin's.

"Thank you so much, sir," Dinah whispered, though relieved, still contrite.

"Please, call me Lazarus."

Christis Christie lives on the east coast of Canada, in Nova Scotia. She gets most excited about diving into a new fantasy world while writing, but also loves a good supernatural plot. Tiss, as she is affectionately called by her friends, enjoys being creative in any way she can, so if she's not writing then she's crocheting or she's embroidering. Her favorite animal is the sloth, and her favorite retellings are anything Beauty and the Beast related.

Blood from a Stone: Villain Anthology

Cirque de vol Mystique: Circus Anthology

Whispered Summons

Heather Karn

1

Great-aunt Cecilia had been dead for nearly two weeks. Apparently she'd lost a battle with some illness I'd never heard of before. As she had no children of her own and had never married, in all her wisdom she'd decided to leave everything to me. Why? Heaven only knew.

And according to Mom, Aunt Cecilia wasn't going to Heaven.

There wasn't much love between Aunt Cecilia and the rest of the family, which was why I stood in her living room with my six-year-old sister, Isabelle, instead of anyone else. I'd been the curious one about Aunt Cecilia's dark magic, and she knew it. Leaving everything to me was a good way to make sure it passed through my hands. It didn't hurt that my parents were both dead and I was a college Junior taking online classes. I could pretty much do as I pleased...as long as it didn't bring harm to Izzy.

Blowing strands of hair out of my face, I sighed as I stared around after my quick tour of the house. There was no distinct foyer. The house opened directly into the living room, with the kitchen and dining room beyond that. Everything my eyes took in was covered in random stuff: boxes, books, knick-knacks, and dust. Lots and lots of dust.

I groaned. This was going to take forever. Most of it was

bound for the town's dump, and whatever was left would go to me to take home or be donated. However, I had to go through all of it to decide which pile it belonged in. Hopefully there weren't roaches and spiders to deal with as well. Just the thought had my skin tingling.

"Okay, Izzy, you're over here today." I set down Izzy's bag of goodies to the left of the door in about the only area that wasn't consumed by Aunt Cecilia's hoarding. "Remember, don't touch anything."

"I know, Meeps," Izzy stated with a hint of aggravation at the constant reminder while using her nickname for me. No one knew why she called me that when my name was Destiny, but she'd started using the nickname the second she could speak and it had stuck.

Without knowing where to start, I crossed the room to a bookcase. Books were my thing, especially when they were books on magic, which these were. Aunt Cecilia had everything, and my sour mood at the job ahead turned to curious investigation. My eyes scanned over the book titles, and a few interested me enough to take them off the shelf and stack them in a pile to read through tonight at the hotel. One in particular caught my eye, and it was my top choice for tonight.

I moved away from the bookshelf to grab an empty box I'd brought and loaded it with more books. Four boxes later, they were stacked in my "keep" pile. There was no way I'd junk or give away books. It was everything else that I wasn't sure about.

Some items were obviously trash, so those were placed into heavy duty garbage bags. Other boxes were filled with items used for casting spells, and I kept those. Spells and potions which used hard to acquire items weren't my strong suit, but I didn't want to throw away perfectly good ingredients in case I ever changed my mind or needed them.

Staring around the room, the thought smacked me in the face that perhaps I was a hoarder like Aunt Cecilia. I shook the thought off as soon as it arrived. I was keeping items I could use, not all this garbage, like a lamp older than me with a torn shade, or an old-style cassette player that likely didn't even work anymore.

The day was long and tedious when I had to sort through junk, which was mostly the right side of the living room. However, some boxes and shelves were fun and held exotic items. When lunchtime came and went, I passed Izzy a jam sandwich and ate one as well. Since I wasn't sure how clean or filthy the house would be before arriving, I'd erred on the side of caution and brought our food and made hotel reservations. Looking at the house now, I was glad I'd decided that.

The sun was setting and my stomach was rumbling by the time I called an end to the day. Not only was I hungry, even with the snacks I'd brought, but my body was sore and my muscles throbbing from crouching, getting up and down, and bending over boxes, as well as lifting them to the different piles. Thus far, I was right: there were far more boxes and bags to throw away than anything else.

"Ready to go to the hotel?" I asked Izzy, who'd been cleaning up her mess of books and toys for the last few minutes.

"Yup," she stated, striding out the open front door ahead of me while I locked it behind us. "Can we have hamburgers for dinner?"

"Yes, ma'am." I led the way to the truck, which had

belonged to my dad before he died, and opened the back cab door behind the passenger seat for her.

After buckling in the little girl, who looked just like me when I was her age with long, sandy blonde hair and bright green eyes, we headed in the direction of town. We made our stop at the one drive-thru restaurant in town and checked into the hotel. It was a small town, so the hotel wasn't part of a large chain, but a locally owned place where the doors open to the outside. Those types always gave me the creeps, but since it was the only one in town, and the next city was twenty minutes in either direction, I sucked it up and checked us in.

While the outside appeared, even in the dark, like it needed a new paint job and the parking lot was chipping away in spots, the inside was far different. I prepared myself for a grungy, smokey scent when I opened the door, but instead, it smelled cleaner than any hotel room I'd ever stayed in. The two queen bed covers appeared new and there wasn't a stain on them. They even smelled fresh and clean. The bathroom was sparkling, allowing me to breathe a sigh of relief.

With Izzy settled at the table in the corner to eat her burger, I carried in our luggage and the small box of books I'd brought back to look at and joined her. The meal was okay, and I forced myself to chew my food and squelch the need to swallow it whole to race to those books. Thankfully she and I both loved books, even at her age, so after dinner, I took one bed and she took the other, scattering books around us.

I started with a book on potions, hoping it might spark something within me to care about that part of magic. It didn't, but I gave it an honest try. The next was a spell book that I'd never studied, for good reason. These spells were dark and dangerous. It wasn't like I was a full-time witch like Mom had been, and the witches and warlocks of the rest of the coven. I practiced magic, but I was likely one of the few witches who didn't like wand waving and all that. I liked the simple spells where I just had to speak a spell for it to work.

Apparently that was why Aunt Cecilia had liked dark magic. It didn't require wands, but it did sometimes need random objects. Those weren't too hard to come by in Aunt Cecilia's house. Plus, wands were so hard to conceal.

The third book, which was the one I'd wanted to pick up first but hadn't wanted to seem too eager, even for me, was a book on demons. However, I was pulled from the book by the loudest six-year-old yawn I'd heard in a long time. Izzy was half sprawled across the bed, her eyelids heavy.

"Okay, Bug, it's pajama time," I announced, reluctantly setting the book aside.

2

With some whining that she was too tired to move, Izzy slid off the bed and followed me to the countertop outside the bathroom where I'd placed her bag. Overall she was a good girl, and I was happy for that. It wasn't easy for either of us right now, but she was a champ. We'd lost Mom and Dad almost a year ago, and thankfully they'd had me listed as Izzy's guardian should something happen to them. Both sets of my grandparents had fought that directive in court, but had lost. Again, I was grateful. Izzy needed me and I needed Izzy, even if life was completely different from everything I'd planned. I wouldn't give her up for any of my old plans.

Teeth brushed and dressed in her jammies, I tucked Izzy into bed after reading her one of the books I'd packed specifically for bedtime.

"Meeps, how long are we going to be here?" Izzy asked as I flicked off the overhead light, the tiny lamp beside my bed the only light to read by now.

I shrugged and kissed her forehead. "I don't know, Izzy. I'm going to try to hurry so we can go home sooner."

"I don't want to go home," Izzy argued, startling me into

turning back to her when I was going to crawl under the covers of my bed.

"Why not?"

"Because it makes me sad. Aunt Cecilia's house is cool."

"You've only seen a few rooms," I argued, sliding under the covers. "How do you know it's cool?"

"Because it's not home," she murmured, squeezing my heart. "Can we move here?"

I'd been trying to talk to her about her feelings since our parents died, but she hadn't said much. Relief swamped me that we were finally getting somewhere. If she kept opening up, maybe I'd be able to avoid the talk of "counseling" that the coven always threw at me. It was one of my grandparents' biggest weapons that they used to threaten me with how they'd take Izzy away from me and show I wasn't competent.

I bit my lower lip. "Umm, let's think on that, okay? We'll explore more of the house tomorrow together and see what we decide. Is that all right?"

"Okay. Goodnight, Meeps. I love you." Izzy rolled over, squeezing her pillow.

"Goodnight, Izzy."

While she fell asleep, I leaned back against the headboard and thought about what she'd said. Since I was finishing college online and also working full-time from home, we could move if we wanted. Aunt Cecilia's house was smaller than the one Mom and Dad had left us, which was fine since it was just the two of us, and it was out of the city. There was a lot of work that needed to go into it first, mostly clearing it out and then cleaning it. The carpets might actually need to be replaced, as well as the threadbare furniture in the living room. I'd taken a short tour upstairs, but I hadn't paid too close attention to what I'd seen. There was so much stuff it was hard to see any of it.

Once Izzy's breathing slowed, I picked up the book on demons and prepared myself to strum through it. The thought of them had always fascinated me. Now was no different.

My first stop was the table of contents. Eyes wide, I skimmed over it, entranced by the ideas I'd never considered, such as more than one type of demon, how to summon them, and uses for demons. There was also a chapter for ways to help your demon blend in with society, and what to do to locate a missing demon, and another on how to send it back to its dimension.

Too curious, I skipped ahead to the demon summoning section, skimming through summoning spells, all in Latin. As a witch, I'd been taught the old language since childhood since most spells used Latin, although the more modern witches were finding ways to intermingle modern words with the Latin.

The dust that had covered the bookshelf and the top of this book was enough to tell me it was an old text, likely one of the first editions, and was printed shortly after the invention of the printing press. However, the information was far older. To preserve it, the witches would've printed this over using hand-written books.

I ran fingers across the yellowed paper, in awe of the text sitting in my lap. The spells ran through my mind, one after another, as I flipped from one page to the next. All they had listed at the top was the name of the type of demon, but since I'd skipped that section, I had no idea what most of them meant.

One particular spell caught my attention, and without

bothering to look at the demon's name, I mumbled the spell from my mouth. It wasn't like it would summon a demon. Those spells were complex, most needing a summoning circle and some of the oddities I'd found at Aunt Cecilia's house. However, the spell left a tingle on my tongue that wasn't altogether unpleasant.

Shaking my head, I blinked my hazy eyes and set the book on the nightstand between me and Izzy. I'd have to wake up early for another peek. There was no way I could keep my eyes open much longer as my vision was blurring with exhaustion.

I slid the rest of the way under the covers after turning my light off. The bed was surprisingly comfortable, far more comfortable than my bed back home, which desperately needed a new mattress. This one was like sleeping on a cloud.

Only partially aware of what was happening around me, I felt the bed dip behind me. Izzy had to be climbing in with me again. It wasn't the first time she'd done it since our parents were killed. It was quite common. Hopefully she stayed on her side tonight and didn't steal the covers.

3

The heat behind me threatened to hold me in sleep's spell, but the hand splayed across my bare stomach said otherwise. My body stiffened. That hand was far too large to be Izzy's, and there was too much heat behind me to be from her tiny form.

Opening my eyes slowly, my gaze landed on Izzy in the other bed, the morning sunlight seeping through the curtains outlining her form and her splay of blonde hair on her pillow. Heart racing, I pushed away, trying to distance myself from the stranger at my back, but his hand held me firmly in place. It was definitely a man as he released a low growl behind me as I tried to pry his large hand from my skin.

"What are you doing?" a deep, gravelly male voice asked, his words slurring from just waking up himself.

What was I doing? Me? What was he doing?

"Who are you?" My voice quivered, and it was a wonder he could hear it at all.

"I'm Cass. Now, lay still. It's barely dawn."

Had I fallen asleep and woken up in some alternate reality where I somehow had a boyfriend or husband? That was the only explanation I had for Cass's calm ease around me, and for his hand lingering against my stomach, his fingers twitching against my skin. Anything else was impossible.

Rubbing a temple, I fought the panic raging inside of me, threatening to overcome my body and mind. I trembled under Cass's hold and swallowed hard to keep bile down. He didn't appear eager to harm me, and certainly if he'd done more than lay a hand on my stomach I would've woken, right?

"Let me up, please," I begged, and with a groan, Cass released me, but didn't move beyond removing his hand from my waist.

The second I was free, I bolted upright and out of the bed, hands balled into fists at eye level, to face the man. His dark eyes scanned my body from top to mid-thigh where the bed hid the rest of me, and back up again. Appreciation sparkled in those inky depths, and I fought a shiver.

It wasn't just a shiver from the way he eyed me. Cass couldn't have been any older than me, not quite mid-twenties, but his hair was stark white, cut short and spiking in every direction on his head from sleep. His skin was nearly as white as his hair, but it had a bluish hue to it that was almost alien, and the muscles pulling taut beneath that skin were the largest I'd ever seen in person. While it was appealing in a masculine way, it was also terrifying to think of what he could do to me with little effort.

If that wasn't bad enough, his short hair revealed sharp-tipped ears, like a mythical elf, but this was no elf. A glint of sunlight through the curtain landed on his face, and before he could move his eyes out of its beam, I gained a clearer view. No, his eyes weren't dark, they were black. Well, except for the whites around them. The iris and pupil had bled together forming an inky orb to clash with his eye's whites.

Then he grinned, one side of his mouth lifting in an arrogant smirk, showing off short fangs instead of incisors. The only thought running through my head was vampire, and I choked on my breath. If he was a vampire, then how was I even still alive? Vamps didn't crawl into witches' beds and spend the night. They killed on sight.

"Uh, who are you, really? Or maybe a better question is, what are you?"

Cass cocked an eyebrow at me, his grin not wavering. "I told you, I am Cass. I'm a Matrada, a Mate demon."

"You're a what?" I screeched, too loud, and my voice caused Izzy to stir. Slapping a hand over my mouth, I stared at the man before me. "What do you mean, 'Mate demon'?"

He tipped his head at me. "You summoned me. How do you not know? It couldn't have been an accident."

The events of last night hit me like a freight train and I had to sit on the edge of the bed or fall over when my legs gave out. It put me closer to Cass, but if he really was a demon, nowhere in this room was far enough away from him. Ignoring the demon, I snatched the book from the nightstand and used the light beyond the curtains to see as I flipped through the pages.

First, I located the spell I'd murmured. Sure enough, at the top of the page was the title "Matrada". I'd inadvertently summoned a demon with little more than a whispered spell. How was that possible? There was no summoning circle, no added items, nothing. I'd been tucked into bed ready for sleep.

Now that I couldn't argue with Cass about me summoning him, and I'd confirmed he was correct, I flipped to the front of the book where the types of demons were listed and sparse information was reported about them. Sparse because some only had their name and nothing about them. A few noted never to summon these demons. Boy, was I glad I hadn't stumbled across their spells. Then again, I hadn't found Matrada demons yet. I crossed mental fingers that his description didn't read the same as those.

It didn't.

It was worse.

Matrada demons, or Mate demons, are one of the few non-hostile demons that exist. While not hostile toward humans, that doesn't mean they aren't destructive in their own right. Most are peaceful, their only desire to be summoned by the witch that will be their mate as there are no female Matrada demons and they are compatible with human witches. It has not been recorded whether offspring of either kind may come of this union, though it is assumed if there is offspring that females are witches and males are Matrada demons. They are also the only demons which cannot be sent back to the demon dimension. Once they have been summoned, the demon will survive until his witch Mate passes, at which time he disappears. No one knows whether they return to their dimension or if they cease to exist once their lover is no longer present in this world.

My eyes were reading, but my brain was having a difficult time believing what was written on the paper. I had to read it over three more times before the truth of the situation started to sink in. By then, Izzy was starting to stir.

The little girl lifted her head and stared at me before her eyes shifted to Cass while I could only sit there with my mouth hanging open. No words of explanation came forth, likely because I was still piecing the whole thing together myself. Just how was I supposed to tell my little sister that I'd accidentally summoned a demon, a demon who was supposed to be my mate?

Mate? Who even used that term anymore?

"Izzy...I can explain," I stammered when she turned wide eyes back on me. "I think."

Gaining strength, I lifted Izzy into my arms and sprinted for the bathroom where I flipped on the light, set her down, and locked the door behind us. It wouldn't stop Cass if he decided he wanted in, but perhaps it was enough of a message I wanted him to stay out that he'd do it. How much of human and Earth life did he know about and how much was I going to have to teach him?

The bathroom was brightly lit and as clean as the rest of the hotel room, which was nice as I crouched before Izzy and took her hands. Her eyes still searched mine for an answer as I tried to think of the right words to say that wouldn't scare her. How could I have been so stupid as to even speak a spell out loud?

4

"Iz, I made a mistake last night, but I didn't know it." I took a deep breath and squeezed her hands, her grip on me almost painful. "Last night, after you went to bed, I was reading through a book on demons, and I happened to murmur a spell. I didn't think anything of it because they're usually complex spells. Well, apparently this is one of the easiest spells, so all you have to do is recite it."

"Meeps, what happened?"

I was avoiding the truth for as long as possible, but it was only upsetting Izzy further. Taking my hands back, I wiped my face and heaved a heavy sigh. This was it.

Meeting Izzy's terrified face, I confessed my sin. "Last night I summoned a demon."

Her mouth popped open. Even young Izzy knew better than to do that. It was dark magic and forbidden by our coven.

"I didn't plan on it," I urged, wanting my baby sister to understand what was happening. "It was a mistake. How was I supposed to know?"

"Is he going to kill us?" Izzy squeaked, her body starting to tremble with the news.

I shook my head. "No, I don't think so. He's not that kind of demon."

Eyes widening further, Izzy gasped softly. "There's more than one type of demon?"

"Apparently so, which is exactly what I was looking at last night," I muttered. "All the spells were so incredibly complex. I just happened to pick the one that wasn't complex to whisper."

"What are you going to do?"

I deflated as a fist banged against the door in a solid knock that made us both squeak, and I grabbed Izzy, keeping myself between the door and her.

"If you didn't want me to hear you," Cass called through the door, "then you should have gone farther away. Why don't you come out and we can discuss this situation together."

There was no hiding my cringe. He could hear me tell Izzy I'd summoned him by mistake? That could only mean he was aware I didn't want him as a mate, that I'd never meant for this to happen. The tension in his tight voice was proof of that.

Izzy and I locked gazes. We didn't really have a choice. Eventually we'd have to make our way out of this bathroom, if only to eat.

After gathering my wits around me so I didn't scare Izzy further, I twisted the doorknob, disengaging the lock. One of us had to be brave, and I refused to let it be the six-year-old. She wasn't the one who'd summoned this demon.

Cass leaned against the wall opposite us beside the counter, gaze dark. I swallowed hard. It wasn't just because of those eyes boring into me, but it was much more the expanse of blue-ish tinged skin that was exposed. There was a lot of it from the waist up. Thankfully a pair of black jeans hugged his waist, even if they did ride low on his hips.

Mouth dry as cotton, I averted my gaze, eyes landing on Izzy's small suitcase on the counter. Mine was shoved underneath out of the way, right next to the demon. There was no doubt in my mind that I'd feel much better about the upcoming conversation if I was fully dressed instead of in my skimpy sleep clothes.

"If you don't mind, Cass, I'd like to clean up before we talk." My words were slow, timid, and soft, like I was waiting for the demon to explode with his wrath at me.

Cass nodded, crossing his arms over his chest, his biceps doubling in size. I swallowed hard at the sight, both terrified and turned on by them. This was ridiculous. There was no way I should be drooling over a demon.

I gave Izzy a nudge back toward the bathroom, and with her gone, I grabbed clothes for both of us. Once the door divided us from Cass again, Izzy and I changed. Since I finished before the girl, I also brushed my teeth and ran a brush through my hair. I'd help Izzy finish cleaning up later.

The demon had moved since I'd shut us back in the bathroom. He sat on the bed where I'd slept, so I led Izzy to her bed, and we sat across from him. The beds were so close, and his legs so long, there wasn't much space between our knees. There was a gap, but I could still feel heat radiating off of him.

Neither one of us said anything, each staring at the other. So, who would break the silence? What would I even say if I did?

In the end, it was Izzy who spoke first.

"What are we going to do, Meeps?" Tears slid down

Izzy's cheeks as her body shook with suppressed sobs. "They'll kick you out of the coven for this. What will happen to me?"

I wrapped my arm around Izzy's shoulders and tugged her against my side. "Hush now. Nothing will happen to you. Do you remember that idea you had last night about us moving here?" She nodded. "Then let's say we do that, shall we?"

It was the only plan that I could think of. She was right in that both sets of our grandparents would seek out the coven leader to banish me from the coven, effectively separating me from Izzy. I'd never let that happen, even if that meant not returning for the rest of our belongings. Nothing in this world was more important to me than Iz.

"Your name is Meeps?" Cass's voice reminded us of his presence, the real reason we were having this conversation. I gave him my full attention and he tilted his head.

"No, not Meeps. It's Izzy's nickname for me. My name is Destiny." I squeezed my sister's shoulders. "Izzy, this is Cass."

Cass's eyes narrowed on me in a dark look. "Your daughter?"

My heart squeezed. Of course he would see it like that. I hadn't given him any reason not to.

"No, my sister. Our parents were killed in a car accident, so I'm raising Izzy."

He nodded, his gaze softening. "That is noble of you."

"No, it's what's right. I love her and don't want anyone to take her from me."

"I heard what you told her," Cass hedged, voice slow and cautious. "You didn't mean to summon me."

"No, and I'm sorry for that. I thought-."

"Like I said, I heard you explain it to the child. However, I can't return to my dimension while you yet live."

What the-? Did he mean? I swallowed hard, Izzy wrapping her arms around me. My other arm crossed in front of her to provide more meager protection.

5

The demon tipped his head again, watching us with open curiosity. "Why the sudden fear of me?"

"Why? You can't return to your dimension with me still alive. That means you plan to kill me, right?"

This time, his eyes flew wide. "I...that's not what I meant. I'd never kill my mate, even if she didn't want me. Why would I do such a thing?"

I shrugged. "I don't know. You are a demon."

"I'm a Matrada."

"That's still a demon, isn't it?"

"Yes, but our craving for blood and violence is nothing compared to our kin. If you asked me never to kill, I would never do it. If you asked me to protect both you and Izzy, I would until my dying breath. If you asked me to think of her as a daughter and help you raise her, I would gladly do so." Cass ran fingers through his unruly, spiky hair. "You think me a monster just because I am a demon?"

His words stunned me into silence. He was looking for an answer, but I had none to give until my brain digested what he'd said. Growing up, I'd been taught that all demons were to be loathed and hated for their violence and evil ways. Never had anyone mentioned that there were demons who would ever be willing to protect...and be willing to raise a child.

"I don't know what to think," I finally admitted.

I wasn't sure how he'd react to the statement, but the tension in his set jaw didn't ease. It didn't grow worse, but it definitely wasn't any better. This was not how I'd planned to start the day.

Rubbing my forehead, I squeezed my eyes shut. "We were raised being taught that all demons are evil. Heck, until last night I only thought there was one kind, and we were meant to believe that they were monsters. It's mind boggling to understand that we were taught wrong."

"You were taught it, yes, but also naive enough to not question it," Cass spat.

His words caused my spine to straighten and my skin to flush with growing anger. "I'm not telling you this so you can insult me. I'm telling you this so that you can understand why I don't know anything else about demons. Our parents taught us about demons, perhaps it was all they were ever taught as well since we were banned from practicing dark magic."

Cass's nose scrunched in disgust. "Dark magic? There's only magic. One kind. Whether or not you use it for evil is up to you. Summoning a Matrada demon is hardly dark."

"Because you aren't evil?" Izzy asked, and I stiffened, her six-year-old mind trying to keep up with the conversation.

My fear-filled eyes met Cass's, and his eyes softened, turning his attention on her. Even his voice was gentler when he spoke to Izzy. Perhaps it was because she was so young.

"I am not evil, Izzy. Destiny didn't tell you what a Matrada demon is, did she?" Izzy shook her head and for a moment I was put out that it sounded like he was throwing me under the bus. "I believe that's because she's still unsure herself. A Matrada is a Mate demon, which may give some connotations Destiny isn't comfortable with.

"We are not evil. While we wouldn't mind killing someone, it's only in defense of the witch who summoned us, and in this case, her family. It means that I am her companion, a friend, a loyal ear to listen to her secrets. I don't have to be anything more than that if she doesn't want me to be. To you, I could be as a father, or a brother, or a friend."

Izzy smiled, her hold on me loosening. "I like that."

I fought not to roll my eyes. Sure, she liked it. The demon hadn't claimed her as a mate. I'd only ever had one boyfriend, and even that hadn't lasted long. Boys were complicated and irritating. Demons couldn't possibly be any better to deal with, especially the half-naked type.

This conversation was giving me a headache. Pinching the bridge of my nose, I sighed.

"Cass, do you mind if we finish cleaning up and then head to my aunt's house to keep sorting through her things? If we're going to be staying here and moving in, I'd like to make it livable soon so we don't go broke staying in a hotel."

Plus, I needed to order new furniture, check out the appliances, buy food for us, and make some sort of plan. I only had a week off from work before I needed to return to it full-time, and then there was college. So far, I wasn't behind, but I would be soon if I didn't keep up with the schedule. How was I ever supposed to do all of this in a week? Less than a week now, actually.

"I will help you," Cass stated, rising from the bed, answering my internal question. "You may not want me as a mate, but perhaps you would allow me the opportunity to prove I am worthy of being a friend?"

There was no way this man was a demon. He was far too sweet. Perhaps I had judged him too harshly for what he was, or what my prejudice against him told me he was.

"Thank you, Cass. That would be acceptable. I could use the help...and a friend."

"Then tell me what it is that you need me to do, and I will do it."

Half an hour later, we piled into my car and headed toward Aunt Cecilia's house. Breakfast, lunch, and dinner would be sandwiches again as they were easy to make at the hotel room. I'd need to buy more bread, though, since I hadn't counted on feeding a demon starting partway through the week.

I cringed at the sight of the lawn and landscaping yet again when we pulled up the driveway. The house sat on three acres of land surrounded by trees, which had also belonged to Aunt Ceclia. However, all three acres of grass resembled a hayfield of tall grasses. It hadn't been mowed all summer, and there were likely dozens of snakes living in it. Since we were out of town and on a back road no one ever used, there were no ordinances that said this mess had to be mowed at all.

"Okay," I sighed, cutting the engine, "let's do this."

Ignoring the bare chested demon beside me, I climbed from the car and helped Izzy out with her bag. More books, coloring pages, and toys would soon litter the ground inside. What greeted us first was the mess from yesterday. Cass stared at the various piles and closed the door behind himself.

"Aunt Cecilia was a bit of a hoarder," I explained, worming my way through the piles and clutter to the kitchen. If we were going to stay here, then I needed to make the most important areas habitable first.

"Yes, it appears that way." Cass followed me, taking in the junk around us. "What would you have me do first?"

6

Stopping, I pivoted and gave him my full attention. "How is it that you know so much about Earth? This dimension, here, whatever you call it."

"Unlike your witches and warlocks who appear too willing to silence knowledge of the other dimension, we seek for any scrap of information we can find. Some use it for dark purposes, planning for the day they may be summoned. Others, like the Matrada, are curious, and wish to be ready for the time that we are summoned as a mate, or in this case, a friend."

"How do you gain your knowledge?"

"From demons who have been returned and...other ways."

That was not comforting. I didn't even want to ask about what other ways demons gained knowledge from a different dimension. My mind was too busy making up its own. None of those were good.

"Okay. Thanks."

With my curiosity settled for now, I focused on the fridge, cringing and ready to tackle the worst case of growing food and leaking containers of my life. Sucking in a deep breath, I held it, peeking inside. Much to my shock, the fridge was practically empty.

The air I'd held rushed from my lungs and I inhaled deep again as I tugged the fridge door open all the way. Pickle jars lined one of the door shelves, with some sticks of butter crammed in a compartment. A few containers sat on shelving inside, and all were growing, but none had leaked or somehow cracked open. Even the drawers were empty.

My sigh of relief didn't go unnoticed.

"Is all well?" Cass appeared beside me, staring at the fridge's contents with me.

"Yes, it's fine. Can you grab that trash can and throw everything in here into it? I'll find a clean cloth and wipe it out. Maybe tomorrow morning we can go shopping for real food to eat." I cast his wide chest a pointed stare. "And perhaps find you a shirt."

Cass chuckled. "I've heard your rules about being fully clothed to enter a building. I find them odd, but I will comply."

They weren't my rules. I didn't mind drooling over the demon cleaning out the fridge. He was a male and he was willingly helping me clean. It didn't get much hotter than that. Neither did those back muscles. I'd never considered that the back could be so toned.

The question of whether or not all demons were as muscular as Cass hovered on the tip of my tongue, but I swallowed it. That might give him the wrong idea. Friends, we were only friends. So, instead, I busied myself with finding a clean cloth and checking on Izzy. The girl was in the same spot as yesterday, coloring.

When my eyes landed on Cass again, I froze, sliding to a

stop. His back was still to me as he pulled the last few items from the freezer, which was also clean. However, it wasn't the fact that he'd taken initiative to check the freezer that stunned me, though it was impressive. Nope, it was the fact he now sported a gray t-shirt over those impressive muscles.

"So, where'd you find a shirt?" I asked, flipping the sink handle to hot water and letting it run until it was warm.

Cass's grin was wicked as his eyes shone with mischief. "Do you remember the 'other ways' I mentioned we received information in the demon dimension? Well, that's how, and no, I'm not telling you. It's a demon secret."

"Fine, keep your secrets, but for that you get to clean the bathrooms." I countered his smirk with a cheeky grin as he arched an eyebrow.

The downstairs bathroom wasn't terrible since I'd cleaned it first thing so we could use it, but I had no idea what the upstairs bathroom, the one that Aunt Cecilia used, looked like. Perhaps there were even two bathrooms upstairs. I couldn't remember. My mind had been too bogged down by all of the junk.

With a sigh, I slammed the water off and propped my arms on the counter's edge and heaved in a heavy breath as anxiety threatened to take me. One job at a time. Just one. I'd forget about the next several on the list and focus on the one.

Large, gentle hands were a comforting weight on my shoulders, grounding me. "I am here to help you, Destiny. Tell me what you need of me and I will do it."

"Why?" My voice quivered as emotions of all kinds stole over me.

"Because, I am your friend. If never anything more than just your friend, I will remain at your side."

"But you want more, don't you?"

He chuckled, leaning in to rub his nose against the outer shell of my ear, causing me to shiver with the husky sound of his voice. "What man wouldn't?" He stood straight, breaking the sensual tension between us. "But I will wait and be patient. Even if you never see me that way, I will still be your friend. Matrada are not only mates, but companions. All we want is to be with our female, in whatever way she will allow."

"That seems a bit desperate."

"It is, I suppose. I've waited nearly a millennia to be summoned, and every second I am by your side is worth that wait. I do not know of any human words that could properly describe what I'm trying to explain."

"I see." I really didn't. I was still too caught up on the fact he'd waited a millennia to be summoned. Just how old was my demon?

My demon. Crap, I was so dead when the coven found out. That meant I needed to hurry up with this house.

Changing my mind, I handed over the cloth and directed Cass to clean out the fridge while I sorted through every cabinet and drawer in the kitchen, including the small walk-in pantry. Most of that food was past its "use by" date, so it wound up in garbage bags.

Izzy joined us at the table a while later to read, wanting to be near us. When Cass took a break from being my gofer running around, he sat beside Izzy and let her read a story to him. He complimented her ability to read, tousled her hair, and assisted me once again with the task ahead of us.

Most of Aunt Cecilia's dishes and random kitchen supplies went in a donation pile, though I kept a few out for us to use now just in case. I'd pack up the kitchen items from home and bring them here soon. They were newer, and I knew where they'd been.

After a quick lunch break, we finished the kitchen and moved upstairs. The condition of the two small bedrooms was as I'd feared: clean, but an inch of dust covered everything, including the beds, dressers, and stacks of boxes. The Master bedroom wasn't nearly in as much neglect, and there weren't nearly as many boxes.

A fourth room was a tiny office. I hadn't done more than peek inside yesterday morning, but now I felt like exploring, Cass at my back. There was a sheet of paper on the desk I hadn't noticed yesterday, so I sat down in the chair and lifted it. Was it being nosy if I was going through a dead woman's belongings that she'd given me?

As it turned out, it was a letter, and it was for me. I swallowed.

?

"My dearest Destiny,

"If you're reading this letter, then I was never able to meet you in person one last time, which is quite the shame. I have always enjoyed your correspondence, though, and your curious mind. This house belongs to you, now, so do with it what you will, but I caution you against selling it. It has been in the family for generations, but only by those of us who practice 'dark' magic. If you are as curious as I think you are, you will find that there are only dark people, not dark magic. It is how magic is wielded that makes it dark. Unfortunately such thoughts and opinions can be detrimental in some circles, like the family coven. Be cautious about that coven. There is more darkness in the hearts of that horde than in a room with no light.

"Keep your sister safe and at your side. The estate lawyer should've given you a key. You'll find the keyhole in the wall beside the painting on your left if you're sitting at my desk. Enjoy this little surprise, and tell no one of its existence. You will know what it is when you see it.

"Love always, Great-aunt Cecilia."

I had to read the letter twice. Once everything had started

to sink in a tiny bit, my gaze lifted to Cass, who'd been reading over my shoulder. Our eyes met, and he shrugged.

"Do you have the key she mentioned?"

"Yes. It's downstairs."

"Shall we figure out what it is she's hidden?"

The question hadn't finished leaving his mouth and I was already moving. Whatever she'd left, it had to be important to keep it hidden and to provide the key to the lawyer to give to me. It was like she didn't want the key and the letter being in the same house just in case the wrong person found it.

Izzy looked at us as I dug inside my purse on the dining room table and pulled the key from one of the zippered compartments. It was an old-fashioned, brass skeleton key. If any key in the world led to a secret room, this would be the one to do it.

We jogged back upstairs, Cass still on my heels with Izzy yelling after us about what we were doing and me calling back to stay there. Not knowing what we'd find, I didn't want her anywhere near it. When Izzy attempted to follow, Cass turned her around. She listened to him. Go figure. Then again, I'd likely listen to a demon too if he ordered me back to my seat.

Back in the office, we searched for the keyhole. Cass was the one to find it at the center of a dark knot in the wood paneling. He had good eyesight because I never would've found it.

Sticking the key inside, I looked up at him towering above me. "Are we ready?"

"Are you concerned?"

His deep voice dripped with worry, and I shrugged. "Not really, but a little."

"Then let me open it."

It wasn't an order, but I relinquished the key all the same and stepped back, peering around Cass but sticking behind his body just in case. In case of what, I couldn't begin to guess. It wasn't like my aunt was going to booby trap the room.

The key clicked in the lock as it engaged, and the panel slid inward. Cass didn't bother checking that I was ready but set his hand on the door and pushed it open slow and steady. The inside of the next room was black until he flipped the light on and stepped beyond the threshold. Confident all was well, he motioned me inside.

Usually in movies that I watched, when there were hidden doorways, they usually led to somewhere techy. Not in this case. My mouth popped open all the same.

"This is Aunt Cecilia's workroom," I stated, staring around at the full shelves, overflowing tables, cauldron, and to my gut-wrenching horror, a summoning circle on the far side of the room. "Why does she have that?"

Warm hands settled on my shoulders. "Remember, not all demons are evil, and most can be summoned and then returned. If you aren't comfortable with it still, also remember that just because it is here, does not mean that you have to use it. Is this room what Cecilia wanted to show you?"

He was right about the demons and summoning circle, and that was comforting. However, I shook my head. "I don't know."

Stepping further into the room, I searched across the tables and shelves. This space was still crammed with items, but they all appeared useful, though some I had to guess at what they were. Cass was able to fill in some of it, like a tiny jar of newt liver.

He scowled when I swatted his hands away from it, a glint in his eyes I didn't like. "Do not open that jar. It probably reeks."

"Not as bad as you might think, and newt liver is quite delicious. In fact, most of the items on this shelf are rarely used in spells."

That caught my attention. "So, what are they used for?"

"They're demon delicacies." His eyes scanned the room. "Are you certain your aunt didn't have a Matrada demon living with her?"

"Why do you ask?"

"Because, those symbols on the book across the room, they're demon tongue, not any Earth language. Only a demon would know those symbols."

I stared at the book he mentioned. "Could a demon have taught her that language?"

"Perhaps, but I don't believe so."

Cass crossed the room to lift the notebook from the table where he flipped pages around and read. Like he'd done to me, I peeked over his shoulder until I caught sight of an envelope with my name on it sitting on the table next to where the notebook had been. I was reaching for it when Cass's voice stopped me.

"How old was your aunt when she died?"

Narrowing my gaze in thought, I lifted the envelope into my hands. "Well, she was significantly younger than grandma, just about a decade older than Mom. So, early fifties I think? She got sick. Why?"

"Because, these ruins, they make no sense as they are. Do you mind if I speculate?"

"You're asking random questions and you've got me curious. Speculate away."

He opened his mouth to speak but caught sight of the envelope. "Never mind. Open that instead. Maybe she'll confirm my theory, or I'm totally off base and you're right."

"Come on, tell me."

Groaning, he set the notebook back down. "Either you're right and she was learning demon symbols, or...she summoned a Matrada demon and had a child with him because this is the same as a child learning to spell your words. But it looks more like a child's hand than an adult."

8

My stomach plummeted at the idea. "If there was a child, where is it?"

He shook his head, staring around the room. "I don't know." After a brief pause, he tapped the envelope. "Open it, and I hope she gave you information to help us figure this mystery out or it's going to drive me crazy."

"You crazy? You're guessing my great-aunt had a baby with a demon. According to the book I read, they didn't think it's possible."

"Oh, it's possible. That book was so old that most of it was speculation. Open that letter."

"Fine. Pushy."

I slid my finger under the adhesive seal, managing to avoid a papercut in the process, and slid out a sheet of fancy stationery. Finding a stool to sit on, I unfolded the paper and read, with Cass again standing behind me. My eyes read, but they were having difficulty believing what they were reading.

"Oh Destiny, if I were alive I'd feel so relieved that you found this letter. I hope you find it in time. There is a reason I chose you to inherit everything. You are not only the most

195

understanding of the witches and warlocks in my old coven, but also the most curious and compassionate.

"You asked me once about demons, and I told you very little. There were too many others around for me to go into detail if one of them should hear me. I didn't want to get you into trouble. Downstairs, there is a book on demons. Perhaps you've already seen it by now. It'll be a start with your learning, but only a start. There is so much about demons that isn't generally known."

I groaned at that. Perhaps I should've explored more before zeroing in on books. Shaking my head, I kept reading.

"This book tells so much of the various types of demons. I need for you to look up the Matrada demon so that you understand the rest of this letter.

"One of my aunts, the one who satiated my curiosity for 'dark' magic had summoned a Matrada demon, and I met him several times. He was the gentlest of males I'd ever met. They were so happy together. So, about a dozen years ago, I was tired of being alone, so I researched Matrada demons and summoned one for myself. Tygen and I were so very happy together. He rarely left my side before I became ill. He's been my shadow since, and it's comforting.

"You are likely wondering why I have given you this letter. Here is the truth, and I hope you are as understanding and compassionate as I believe you are: Tygen and I had a child together, a little boy, a demon. If this bothers you, I'm sorry, but I need you to keep reading. Lars was born nearly seven years ago, just before your mother had Isabelle. He's a good boy and stays out of trouble. Tygen was trying to teach him all he could about being a demon for the time Lars is old enough to return to that dimension. I don't understand it fully, but since Lars was born here, he can cross between dimensions at will. Apparently most Matrada demons prefer to remain in their dimension so that they have a chance to be summoned. They can't be summoned to their mate if they're already in this dimension.

"I'm likely overloading your mind with information, but there is a little left. You're likely wondering where Lars is and what this has to do with you. I'm sorry to put a burden on you, more than there is already, but Lars is still young, only a child, and he needs to be cared for. I pray you'll help me with this and raise him like you are Isabelle. There is money in my bank account that you have access to that should help provide for him until he reaches maturity and can cross if he wishes. He will be little trouble, and easy to disguise in public should you want to take him anywhere.

"Now, as to his location. If you've been over the rest of the house you can see he isn't there. Across the room, on the opposite wall of where you entered is another keyhole for the key that got you in here. This will lead you down a secret staircase to the basement of this home. This was where we lived most of our lives, away from the prying eyes of other witches, like your coven. It is completely furnished and this is the only entrance. Lars is down there, and he has enough food for a few months, so I hope you heeded my first letter to the lawyer to visit my home early.

"Please, do not be afraid of Lars. He wouldn't hurt you. Yes, he is a demon, but Matrada demons are peaceful, except when those they love are in danger. You should note that the book doesn't tell you what their powers as demons are, so I will. They are strong, far stronger than anyone I've ever seen. While their skin has a blue hue to it, they have the ability to shift that skin tone to blend in with their surroundings. They also, once summoned, have the ability to learn to use your magic, syphoning it through your connection. You can block this, but I found with Tygen he only used my magic when he was curious, and not for malicious intent.

"I'm sorry for the length of this letter, but there is so much more that I want to say and there isn't time and I don't have the energy. Tygen has chosen to join me in the afterlife instead of returning to his dimension. Already I miss Lars, and yet he sleeps beside me now, using my lap as a pillow. There are only a few days left. Please, Destiny, please give my baby a hug for me, please hold him tight and tell him I love him. Please, please have mercy and care for him. It shouldn't be your burden, but I can think of no one else who I would trust with this task.

"I love you, Destiny, and good luck. Love, Aunt Cecilia."

I swallowed hard. "You were right, Cass. There is a child."

"And he's likely afraid." Cass left my side to stare at the far wall, the one with the entrance to the basement. "We should find him."

"We will." I joined Cass at the wall and took one of his hands, startling him to look down at me. Shrugging, I stared back at the wall. "You seemed upset, so I thought holding your hand might help."

"Oh. Well, I'm interested in the child's well-being."

"Do all Matrada demons care about children this much?"

"We care very much for our mates and our young, even the young of others. If you are to raise this boy like you are Izzy, then I will do so at your side." He pressed his lips together, pondering his next words. "Matrada demons are...we have a strong natural desire, instinct even, to protect those we see as ours, our family. We also feel this way toward young, whether ours or another's. I cannot describe it any other way. If you choose to take on this responsibility, you will not be doing it alone. I will help, and I'll help Lars be ready to enter the demon dimension when he is old enough and wishes to do so."

I squeezed Cass's hand. "Thank you. In so many ways, you're much better than many of the human men that I know."

9

"Let's find that keyhole," Cass murmured, as if my words had affected him more than he wanted me to know. "That child has been alone long enough."

He was too right about that. Both of our attention fell on the wooden wall, and I also swiped my hand across it, trying to feel for the keyhole. In the end, it was Cass who once again found it. I wanted to smack the satisfied grin off his face, but instead rolled my eyes at the man. It may have only been a few hours since we'd met, but there was something about him that drew me to Cass. That something was both terrifying and exhilarating.

The doorway clicked open toward us, revealing a dark staircase. As before, Cass found the light switch and led the way ahead of me, his protective nature not wanting to put me in harm's way. The further down we walked on the spiral staircase, the more my stomach twisted. What condition, physically, mentally, and emotionally, would this boy be in when we found him?

Another door blocked our way at the bottom, but this one wasn't locked. Cass gave me a nod over his shoulder before twisting the handle and entering a brightly lit room. He stepped in, surveyed the area, and moved aside to reveal an empty room. Well, empty of people. There were plenty of furnishings. It was like a whole different house had been built below the upper levels.

"Lars?" I called into the room, voice barely louder than a whisper.

No one responded, so I stepped further into the living area. A kitchen could be seen through a large opening in the left wall, making it both a bar to eat at and a way to pass food into the living room, which also had a dining room table off to the side. More doorways led off to the right, which I assumed were bedrooms and a bathroom.

A few more paces into the room, I halted. I'd heard something, but I wasn't sure what or where. Holding still, I listened harder, but nothing.

"Lars? It's Destiny. Aunt Cecilia told me about you. Will you come out?"

Still nothing.

I opened my mouth to call again, but Cass covered it with his hand with a gentle touch. "He won't come out like this. Let's just wait. Keep the door open and see what he does."

Crossing my arms, I shook my head in irritation, mostly with myself that I couldn't get this boy to come to me. "Cass, what's the demon dimension like? Do you mix and mingle with other demons? Did you know Tygen?"

"It's possible," Cass stated, crossing his arms. "Tygen is a popular name among Matrada demons, so I may have known him since I knew a few that were summoned. As for what it's like, it's much like Earth, but different. Our homes are not like this, and our plants are different, and we don't have jobs like humans do, but we have gatherings and parties, provide food for ourselves and others, and we work for what we want. It's simpler, much simpler. That's not to say human life is better or worse compared to demons. It's just different."

A question burned on the tip of my tongue and I bit my lip to silence it. Until I couldn't. "Cass, when you teach Lars about demon symbols and about the demon dimension, am I allowed to learn as well?"

He arched a brow at me. "Are you sure you want me to?"

"Yes. I may have feared demons before, but that's because my coven lied and hid the truth. I'm done hiding from it. I want to know. If that means moving here to keep us all safe, I'll do it. If it means keeping an open mind, I'll do that too. Please, Cass."

"Hmm. I guess we could try it. First, let's work with Lars and finish this house."

I nodded. He was right. We had priorities.

Staring over the room again, I contemplated searching it for Lars, but shook my head. He'd come out when he was ready. We were new faces he didn't know. I'd be scared of us too if I were him.

"Yeah, let's go upstairs and clean."

"Mama always kept it cluttered so people wouldn't come in and stay," a tiny voice spoke from behind the couch across the room. "She said it was safest."

My heart twisted at the sound of the boy's trembling voice. "Yes, but if I move in here and don't clean it up, someone will notice," I countered, voice soft and gentle. "Plus, I want to make the upstairs usable for my sister. Would you like to meet her? She's about your age."

A white haired, bluish skinned head stuck itself out from between the couch and wall, black eyes wide. They widened further when they landed on Cass. The adult demon, previously a mountain of intimidation, crouched low to the ground, resting his forearms on his thighs.

"You're safe, Lars," Cass stated. "We won't harm you. We are family."

Lars's throat bobbed as he swallowed. "You're like me and Papa?"

"A Matrada demon? Yes. Recently summoned from the demon dimension."

"And you're a witch?" Lars rested his gaze on me, and I nodded.

"Yes, I am, and so is my sister, though neither one of us practices magic much."

"Mama used to make potions and enchantments for other witches. She was always using her magic." The boy slid out from behind the couch, barely larger in form than Izzy. "If you wanted, I'm sure she wouldn't mind if you used her workroom."

I smiled at the boy and reached out a hand. "I'm sure you're right. Are you hungry?"

He shook his head. "No, there's some food down here." That didn't stop him from taking my hand as he stared at Cass, who was on eye level with him and a foot away. "Are you two mates like Mama and Papa?"

"Yes," Cass stated without question or hesitation. "Mates and friends."

10

Izzy's eyes widened the second we appeared in the main house's kitchen minutes later with Lars in tow. The two kids greeted one another, and Izzy instantly handed Lars her second coloring book and crayons. It didn't seem like he'd done much coloring, but Izzy's chatter and questions had them both distracted soon after while Cass and I continued to work on the main house.

"Should we be changing things if Cecilia had them like this as a front?" Cass asked as I handed him a box of kitchen supplies to add to the donation pile. The kids grew quiet, listening for my response.

I shrugged. "I think of it this way: in a game of tag, you can't keep hiding in the same spot or hiding in similar places or people are going to become suspicious and find you and know where you're hiding. Plus, it would be weird to move into someone else's house and keep it the same as they had it. That would draw more attention than hide us."

Cass bit his lower lip, thinking on my words, then nodded. "I suppose that's true. I never thought about it that way. If someone who'd visited her before came now-."

"They'd wonder why I still have her clutter around and where my stuff is at. We can still keep the front that this is the main house, for whatever reason Aunt Cecilia did it, and keep the basement a secret, but we can't keep this area the same. Plus, I can't live underground. It would drive me crazy."

"That would do the same to me as well, I believe," Cass stated, crooked grin on his face. "I'll put this where you need it."

While Cass did as I asked, I turned my attention on Lars, who still watched me. "Does that make sense?"

"I guess so. Do you need help?"

Lars was a sweet little seven-year-old. I liked him already, and my heart hurt for him, as it did for Izzy. Neither of them should grow up without parents. Cass entered the room again, setting hands on his hips to survey what was happening.

Decision made, I strode over to him, grabbed his arm and hauled him after me to the living room and out the front door. The driveway was gravel, and the stones crunched under my shoes as I headed toward the end of it so there wasn't a chance we could be overheard.

"What's wrong?" Cass asked, picking up on my anxiousness.

I stopped walking, intertwining my fingers together as I gazed out at the trees across the street from Aunt Cecilia's house. "Do you really mean what you say? That you'll help me raise the kids?"

"Yes, of course. I'm your mate. If you view them as yours, then so do I. Destiny, what's this about? What's wrong?"

Still jittery, I faced him. He stood so close. I hadn't realized how close until then. His heat filled the gap between us, and I took his hands to steady mine. Taking a breath for courage, I met Cass's gaze.

"I can't raise them alone, Cass, and I will raise them, both of them. But I'm afraid. Some days I still feel like a kid myself. If you're here to stay, then I need you, I need your help. They need a father figure as much as they need me. I know this is crazy, and we practically just met, but if you do this, I promise to be your mate, not just your friend. It'll just take time."

Cass released my hands to cup my face with his, the warmth a soothing balm to my fears. "Destiny, I am a demon. Human laws and instincts don't guide me. Matrada demon instinct is to love and protect our families. The moment you summoned me, you became my family, and your sister is mine, and that little boy is family. You have my support. I swear it. And I promise to do what I can to help raise them well, both of them.

"As for you being my mate, that has always been the case. Neither you nor I can change that fact. In time, you'll see it as I do, and I'm patient enough to wait for it. You do not have to give your body to me, ever, if you don't wish it. I will not take it if I know you aren't ready, and you're nowhere near ready, and I wouldn't expect you to be. I am still a stranger to you. This is not a trade, Destiny. I'm not helping you raise those children in exchange for sharing your bed as more than a friend. That is not how this works. Ever."

Tears slid down my cheeks to wet his hands. "Thank you, Cass. Thank you so much."

He leaned in, his soft, hot lips searing my forehead with a gentle kiss. "You have nothing to thank me for. Will you please tell me your plan?"

"Clear everything out that we can and then go back home to grab the few essentials we left behind since we weren't expecting to stay."

"Back to your coven?"

"Yes. If we're fast and quiet, they won't even know that we're there. I wish I could go alone-."

"I'd never let you."

"But we can't leave the kids alone, which means we're going to have to bring them. I need your strength for a few things of Mom's I want to bring back."

"I'll help." Cass released my face to grab one of my hands and squeezed it. "Let's go clean this house for you."

"First, let's eat dinner. I'm starving."

Cass led me back to the house, my hand in his. In all my life I'd never felt so protected and cherished, and I hoped I'd never take it for granted. Perhaps there was something about this Matrada demon that had my human instincts all confused. While I didn't love Cass, there was definitely quite a bit of affection.

We spent the rest of the day cleaning and sorting on the main level. Tomorrow I'd need to haul the garbage to the local dump so we had more room. Then I could also take a load to be donated.

That night, when I announced it was time to leave for the hotel, Lars stopped me. "Why do we have to go? Can't we stay downstairs?"

His words halted me. I hadn't thought about it. My brain was on auto-pilot and it knew the hotel was our home away from home because this place was a disaster.

Except downstairs wasn't.

I looked to Cass. He lifted one shoulder in a lazy shrug,

his inky black eyes sparkling with curiosity about what I'd decide. It was an easy decision, but I still didn't make it lightly. My two demons would be safest here.

11

"Yes, we'll stay here, but…" I looked to Cass, who tipped his head at me. "If we go back to my place tonight, we can grab everything we'll need now and no one will be looking for us. We've only been gone a couple days. If we wait, they'll be expecting us to return."

Cass nodded. "How long will it take to reach your home?"

"A few hours. Well, four. It'll be the dead of night so no one should even notice us. The kids can sleep in the car." I only had one booster seat in the truck, but something told me my Matrada demon cousin would be just fine on impact if what the book and Aunt Cecilia said was true. "We'll grab our belongings from the hotel on the way back."

"That's good. Okay, children, let's go on an adventure," Cass stated, beckoning the children toward the front door.

I grabbed my purse from the table and followed them outside, locking the door behind us. On a whim, I'd left the skeleton key hidden in a junk drawer inside. It wasn't the basement I didn't want anyone to touch. It was Aunt Cecilia's workroom. Something told me I'd be spending a lot of time in there soon finding out what this "dark" magic was all about.

Cass had the kids strapped in the back when I arrived, so I climbed into the driver's seat and readied to go while he finished up and took his seat behind me. Already the sun was setting, which meant this journey would be made completely in the dark both ways. I hated driving in the dark, but it was our best chance of not being spotted.

"Is four hours far enough away from your coven for us to be safe?" Cass murmured a couple hours later after the kids had both fallen asleep. It had taken Lars far longer to crash because he'd never left the house and the world was all new to him. The newness and excitement hadn't been strong enough in the end to ward off sleep.

"It's going to have to be. I don't know how to spell a house to move it."

Reaching between us, Cass took the hand I rested on my thigh. "Then I will keep you safe if anyone comes."

I smiled up at him. "I know you will, Cass. I trust you."

"And I trust you."

Two hours later, we pulled into the subdivision where my parents, and a large part of our coven, lived. Most of the houses were dark, affirming my theory that this was the best time to do our packing and leaving. Even still, my skin crawled from a feeling of being watched, but I didn't see anyone.

"Let's do this as silently as possible," I whispered after I'd backed into the garage and shut the door. It was useless to whisper, but I still felt creeped out. Cass nodded, understanding my need for quiet.

We left the kids in the cab sleeping. They knew where we'd be if they woke up and needed us. So, I led Cass to the adjoining door of the house.

It was silent inside, Cass leading the way as usual. I'd made a mental list of all that I wanted to grab, and I prayed it fit in my truck.

The first stop was my room where I grabbed out a few suitcases and dumped my clothes and toiletries in without care, and a few pictures ended up in the mess. My next stop was Izzy's room. While Cass helped a little with the task, he spent most of his time listening and watching since I didn't really need him yet. Once all the suitcases were full, I had him take them to the garage.

Next was Mom and Dad's room. I'd gotten rid of most of their belongings after they'd passed, but kept all that I'd wanted. These were already packed in boxes and totes, which I'd yet to take to the basement because I couldn't stomach it. So, Cass took those to the garage as well.

I stopped at the linen closet and grabbed up as much bedding and towels as would fit in a tote I dumped out in my room which held old clothes. Bathroom belongings ended up in a box. I cringed when I checked the time. We were taking far too long.

Skipping the rest of the bedroom things, I moved to the kitchen, packing up everything that I wanted. It was yet again surprising how little fit inside one box or tote, but I used as much space as I could find. When Cass warned me we were running out of room, I had a moment of panic.

"It's all right," Cass stated, resting his hands on my shoulders. "We can always come back."

"I don't want to." I shook my head, punctuating my argument. "I never want to come back here again."

"Then only take what you will regret leaving. If we have

the funds, we can purchase new later, or use what Cecilia has until we can afford new."

I nodded. He was right. So, I finished packing up what things were most important, including crucial documentation and the one thing I wanted above all: Mom's sewing machine. My skills lacked in the ability to sew, but this was Mom's most prized possession, and I had hours of memories just watching her sew in the evenings while I read books. The books also got packed.

Job complete, we climbed back into the truck, our doors slamming making the kids stir, but neither one opened their eyes as we headed out of town. We'd done it. We'd snuck in and snuck out without notice. I'd say it was too easy, but really, it wasn't like anyone was expecting us back yet. And if they found us, I'd just easily say I was leaving the coven. It wasn't like they could stop me.

The horizon was already changing colors to a bright orange by the time I swung the truck into the hotel parking lot. Once the engine cut, I turned in my seat to find four blurry eyes staring at me from the back seat. Either stopping had woken the kids or they'd woken up earlier and weren't chatty.

"I'll be right back," I told them, voice low. "I'll grab our things and then we'll head home and you can go back to sleep if you want."

Izzy turned in her seat and leaned her head against the window. Lars nodded, closing his eyes with a deep breath. They really were great kids. How'd I end up lucky enough to raise them?

"Do you need help?" Cass murmured, and I shook my head.

"No, I should be able to manage it. There's not much there. Stay with the kids."

I was ready to fall asleep myself as I climbed from the truck and swiped the keycard over the door. However, that exhaustion evaporated the second I stepped a foot into the hotel room. Two women occupied the private space inside, both of whom I knew well.

12

"What are you doing here?" I ground out to my grandmas.

"We came to see if you needed any help," Grandma Phillips stated from the far side of the room.

Grandma Kentwood sat on the bed, a book in her hand...the same book I'd used to summon Cass. "Then we found this. Destiny, what are you doing with this? If Cecilia's house is full of dark magic, then you need to leave it as is and sell it."

"First, you two shouldn't be in here. Second, you have no right to go through my things. And third, I'll do whatever I feel is best for me and Izzy. This is stalking."

"We're only looking out for your future in the coven," Grandma Phillips stated, drawing closer.

I lifted a hand. "Yeah, about that. I'm tired of being controlled by our coven. If you two don't leave now, I'm leaving the coven. Permanently. And I'm taking Izzy with me."

Two pairs of burning eyes glared back at me.

Grandma Kentwood found her voice first. "You wouldn't dare. If you do, we'll take her from you."

"You can't. That's called kidnapping, and what are you going to tell the judge? That we're witches and we left your precious coven? That's laughable. Now, give me my things and get out."

The book snapped shut as Grandma Kentwood stood up. The second she was on her feet she stiffened, eyes frozen on something behind me. I could feel him without even looking. Cass stood in the doorway, and he had both witches' attention as their mouths fell open.

"You've already performed dark magic," Grandma Phillips breathed, taking a step back.

I shrugged. "On accident, but I don't regret it. Plus, I'm learning that there really isn't anything as 'dark' magic. It's only dark when used for evil purposes. This demon is actually sweet and helpful, and he wouldn't hurt a fly unless it meant to harm me. Now, will you leave?"

Both women nodded, their fear palpable, even though they were two powerful witches. Their fear of demons was placed in lies and hidden truths. I almost felt sorry for them and their ignorance.

"You won't have time to leave the coven," Grandma Kentwood spat as she neared the doorway and Cass stepped further into the room to give the women space to leave. "Once we tell the leaders what you've done, they'll banish you. We'll be back for Izzy."

"No, you won't," Cass growled, voice a deep, threatening rumble. Sparks erupted around his hands, and I felt a tug on my magic. Did he even realize what he was doing?

My grandmas noticed, and both scurried from the room. It was one thing to face down a demon. It was another to face that same demon who had access to magic. I'd need to talk to Cass about this, but now wasn't the time.

"Go back out," I urged. "I'll only be a second. Don't leave Izzy alone." I didn't dare speak Lars's name.

Cass nodded and fled the hotel, the truck door closing seconds later. With only me in the room, I spoke a spell that would neutralize any spells that my grandmas would've placed in the room. Or, I hoped it would. I wouldn't have put it past either woman to spell something of mine or hide something they spelled to do harm or listen in on me.

For security purposes, I performed the spell two more times. Three was a lucky number, right? It had to be now.

Grabbing everything I could find, I shoved them into the nearest bags and suitcases. In the end, everything fit nicely inside and I left the room. Cass met me just outside and grabbed the bags, eyeing a car further down the line.

"Is this it?"

"I have to go check out," I stated, handing off the bags. "Otherwise I'll keep having to pay for the room."

"Go quick. They're still here."

My nerves were almost shot when I reached the hotel lobby at the end of the row of doors. I wasn't too far away from the truck, but I was far enough that I worried what one of my grandparents would do if I was out of sight for too long. I didn't worry for Izzy, or for Cass, but if they didn't know about Lars, I wanted to keep it that way.

The checkout process seemed to take forever, even when the desk clerk noticed my anxiety-induced bouncing. I swore he took longer just for that. In hindsight I should've brought Cass with me to hurry this man up. Then again, he might've wet himself in the process of helping me if Cass were here.

Receipt in hand, I jogged back to the truck and climbed inside, the keys still in the ignition from when I'd left minutes before. Cass kept his gaze on the cars in the parking lot while I backed out and burned rubber leaving the parking lot. Not that there was any traffic on the road, but I wanted to get away from there as fast as the truck could take us.

I'd expected my nerves to settle the further we drove from town, but they didn't. Every few minutes I checked the rearview mirror, expecting to see someone tailing us, but there was no one. It didn't help that Cass was tense and silent at my side, until he finally spoke up.

"Do you know how to ward?" Cass asked, jaw clenched and his teeth grinding together.

"Yes, that's the one spell I excel at." I grinned, still tense but needing an outlet for it. "Let's just say I was an extremely private teenager."

"Good, because I don't think they're just going to leave us alone now."

"They will once they come against my wards, and with you here, they won't dare come alone."

"There were men in the car with the women."

"Even with my grandpas, they won't dare come against us." Or so I hoped and told myself.

"Good. Let's hurry then."

I glared out the windshield, keeping my eyes on the road and the rising sun. "I'm already speeding. I don't dare go any faster."

By the time we reached the house, my new home, I was trembling. That had been the worst twenty minutes of my life. I wasn't sure what I expected my grandparents to do, which was part of the problem.

"Take the kids inside and downstairs," I ordered Cass as I backed the truck up the driveway. "I'll ward the property and then we can unload everything."

13

Cass did as I ordered while I went in search of salt in the second pantry, which I hadn't investigated yet, in the kitchen. It held plenty, as though Aunt Cecilia warded the house herself quite often.

Racing back outside, I started pouring the salt over the ground and murmuring the chanting spell that would set up the ward. I strode around the entirety of the treeless property, snakes and all, continuing the spell. For good measure, I rounded the property twice.

"It's done," I announced to Cass, who stood beside the truck watching me work. "All they'll find is a vacant lot and they won't be able to step foot inside because of the horde of snakes that they'll find in the grasses."

Cass eyeballed the grass beside the house with a smirk. "That's not a far fetched idea."

"Exactly why I chose it."

My grin faded a second later as a familiar car rounded the corner, coming into view. I snatched up Cass's hand and squeezed it tight, my heart constricting in much the same way. We were about to find out if my ward making skills were any good after all.

"It's all right," Cass murmured into my ear as the car slowed to a stop and a man stepped out.

Grandpa Phillips was a tall, lean man, the nicest of the four of my grandparents, but not by much. While they all liked one another, they hadn't been happy with my parent's union, thinking that they could've done better marrying stronger magic holders.

I held my breath as he stepped toward the lot. However, when his eyes widened and he hustled back to the car, I breathed a sigh of relief.

"How long will it take them to realize that's only a ward?" Cass asked, concern in his voice as the car sped further down the road.

"I don't know. My wards are pretty convincing." I winked at Cass, muscles easing for the first time in hours. "I fooled my parents quite a bit, and they knew me well. Those four will probably think they took a wrong turn somewhere. I think for now, we're safe."

Cass's grin grew wider as he turned his attention from me to the house. "Welcome home, Destiny."

"Welcome home, Cass. What do you say about just leaving the truck bed loaded for now and finding a bed to crash on for a few hours?"

His eyebrows rose. "Bed? As in singular?"

I shrugged. "If you keep your hands to yourself, you're welcome to join me. It's that or the couch. Take your pick."

He chuckled. "You go lay down. I need far less sleep, so I'll unload the truck bed, and then I'll join you."

While a bit of guilt twisted my insides, Cass was adamant that he wanted to do this and that I needed sleep. We were both right; I did. Already I was dizzy and ready to fall over. I hadn't pulled an all-nighter in quite some time.

The kids were downstairs at the table coloring when I emerged from the stairway. They smiled and waved, both wide awake after a night's sleep in the car. After making them promise to be good, I found the basement master bedroom and flopped on the bed. I didn't even care if the bedding was clean or not. It was soft, and it was comfortable.

Twenty minutes later, the bed dipped behind me and a masculine sigh filled the room. I reached behind me, grabbed Cass's arm and draped it over my side. He splayed his hand over my shirt across my stomach, much like he had yesterday morning when we'd woken.

"You're supposed to be asleep," he mumbled, then yawned, burying his face in my long strands of hair. "Go to sleep."

"I was trying, but my brain won't turn off. It's like I'm too tired to sleep."

"There's no such thing. Sleep."

We were silent for a few minutes and I couldn't keep my words in any longer. "Cass?"

He grunted in reply.

"What happens to demons when their mate dies?"

He groaned and held me tighter. "They have the option to choose between staying with their love's soul after death or returning to the demon dimension. Most go with their love. Few return."

"Do they regret that choice?"

"Some do. However, if they return, they can be summoned again as a mate for a witch."

I bit my lip, afraid to ask but needing to know. "If I died right now-?"

"I'd go with you," Cass interrupted. "I will never leave you alone. I promise."

My heart tightened. "We need to find a witch or warlock we trust, one with a Matrada demon."

"Why?"

"So if we die, the kids have someone to take care of them."

Cass flinched behind me and pulled me against his chest. "We will. Now sleep. Neither one of us are dying in the next few hours. You need your energy to clean upstairs. It's still a mess."

It was my turn to groan. "You know what?"

"What?" he chuckled, the deep sound curling my toes.

"I'm glad that I whispered that spell. I'm glad that I have you."

"As am I, Destiny. As am I. Now sleep."

"Are all demons this bossy?" My question was punctuated by a deep yawn.

"Yes, especially a Matrada demon with an obstinate mate."

"Good night, mate."

"Good night, my Destiny."

About Heather

Heather is a lover of all books YA Paranormal Romance and Urban Fantasy, but it wasn't until she was in college that she realized this. It's likely why the book she wrote in 8th grade was rewritten several times and then set aside to sit on her bookshelf to never see the light of day. Once Heather found the genre that she enjoyed above all others, she dove back into reading, and with it, writing. That's why even her Christmas books are filled with dragons and shifters.

Second Lineage

Third House

Zero Tolerance

Fourth Bunker

Negative Energy (Coming September, 12 2020)

Die from a Broken Heart

Elle Beaumont

1

The alarm on Seth's phone plays a tinkling song, the same annoying jingle he refused to change. It was the only sound that cut through his deep sleep. Usually, I can ignore it since it isn't *my* alarm, but today I'm up long before it goes off. I already made coffee for Seth, because today he's on his way to South Carolina with his film crew.

About six months ago, he landed a filming deal for his job as a Ghostbuster—or, as normal people call it, Supernatural Investigator. Seth travels around a lot due to the filming locations, and I remain at home, mostly. Sometimes I go with him. I have fun watching him in his element, but lately, things are strained. He's distant, barely talks, and I'm scared this is the end for us.

I should stay in Churchville, Virginia, but I won't. Instead of letting him make the trip to Russell, South Carolina by himself, I figured I'd enjoy the road getaway with him, and hopefully close whatever distance grew between us. He has interminable days filming, and I work at an animal hospital as a receptionist. Days off together—let alone an entire week— are scarce for us, but that's why I'm going with him.

Once Seth is out of bed, I hear him rummaging around in the kitchen.

"I didn't set the coffee," Seth murmurs.

"I did." I stride into the kitchen and wrap my arms around his waist. "So you could make a travel mug to go, if you wanted."

Seth shrugs out of my arms and looks down at me. "You don't have to do this."

"But I want to. Seth, whatever is going on between us, I want to work this out with you—with us."

Seth nods and combs his fingers through his shaggy blond hair. His blue eyes, which usually hold laughter, are dark with a sadness I wish I understood. If he'd talk to me, we could sort this out, but a twist in my gut warns me what is about to come.

"All right, all right. Time to move."

Seth grabs a travel mug, filling it with coffee, and heads toward the living room where all the bags are. In a moment, the front door softly closes.

A soft trilling meow snags my attention. Snuffy, our orange tiger cat, winds around my legs. I crouch down and rub his head, then under his chin. Apparently, it isn't enough. Snuffy stands on his hind legs to whuffle my face, then scrapes his cheek against mine.

"I'll miss you, too." I give him a peck on the head and turn around. "Hey babe, I'll be right out there. I'm just leaving a note for Stacey for when she comes to take care of Snuffy." Finishing, I give Snuffy one more kiss before walking out of the house.

Seth is busy loading the trunk. As he hurls his bags into the car, the same sinking feeling in my gut tells me things won't fix themselves. If only I knew what I did or where we went wrong.

I met Seth shortly after graduating from college, and I

started working at the animal hospital. His blue eyes were full of tears as he approached the receptionist's desk; he held a cat carrier, and an old feline yowled inside. The cat's appointment wasn't a checkup, but euthanasia. I offered him comfort. And after that, the rest, as they say, is history.

Stop thinking like that, Abs. You'll just get yourself in a tizzy.

Before we leave for South Carolina, Seth goes through his typical checklist, and I stand there wishing he glances my way with his crooked smile—or anything to give me hope we'll be back to normal soon.

He doesn't. He unzips his camera bag, muttering, then tosses it in the back seat. Another mumble, then Seth throws the last bag into the trunk of his Corolla and shuts it.

"I haven't been on a hunt with you in a while," I say, stepping around the car to the passenger side.

When I joined him in the past, I rarely went to the location. I was a tourist in whatever area we landed in. I'd explore the town or city, find the best restaurants, and enjoy my time. On the rare occasion I went to the site, I stayed out of the way until they finished filming.

Seth says nothing, but glances in my direction and nods his head before climbing in the driver's seat. He dials in the address and peers over at me again. "It'll take six hours to get there."

"I guess it's a good thing I didn't sleep well last night."

I didn't sleep at all, actually. Most of the night had been spent curled up on the couch watching TV. *I Love Lucy* reruns kept me company last night until the wee hours of the morning. Surprisingly, I wasn't tired, but I knew I could sleep in the car, anyway.

Seth whips his phone out, hooks it up to the USB cord and sets it in the stand. His hand hovers over the device, eyes glued to the screen as he goes over his road trip playlist.

Playfully, I swat him out of the way to pull up some tunes. He glances in my direction, surprise flickering in his gaze. I put one of my favorite songs on and settle in for the next six hours.

"What was that?" he asks.

"A love tap." I grin and close my eyes, leaning against the car window. Now we're ready for the road trip.

Hours pass by, as do the miles. At one point, I think I fell asleep. I'm not sure, because I don't recall my eyes ever closing. The scenery differs from the highway by the time I wake up, which means we're passing through a small town, or we're at our destination.

Finally, Seth pulls into a gas station. I stare at the GPS, which says we're in Russell, South Carolina, and we're only a few minutes out from Green Meadow Inn.

When I stir, Seth glances my way, his gaze lingering for a moment. Whatever tension I thought we'd leave behind in Virginia is still here. The uneasiness between us is nearly tangible, almost as heavy as the humid air rushing into the car as he exits. I sigh, sitting there, listening to the twang of country music blaring from the radio above the pump.

"Do you think we can talk about what's going on? Whatever this is?"

Seth slides into the driver's seat and we're off again. The sun was out in Virginia, but as the miles pass, and the day drags on, mugginess meets us. At least the thick blanket of clouds wards off the sun... I don't think I could bear the humidity *and* the heat at once.

He stares ahead, only taking his eyes off the road to glance at the GPS. "Not now, please. Not now."

My heart plunges to my stomach. All I want is for things to return to normal. Seth has always been fairly interesting. He has a darker sense of humor, a quick wit, and he's always the first to drag me into a fresh adventure. That's how I fell in love with him. But lately he's withdrawn, closed off, his humor gone. I realize it's only a matter of time before we sit down and hash things out, and that a breakup is around the corner. As much as it'll burn, anything is better than the unspoken tension between us now.

Siri demands we take a right on Willow Drive. Out of the few streets we've passed in Russell, this is likely the most picturesque town I've ever seen—like something out of a Nicholas Sparks movie. Gorgeous old houses with white picket fences line the streets, and massive old oak and maple trees tower over the sidewalks.

"Ready or not," Seth murmurs, surprising me.

"Why wouldn't I be?" I press, glancing at him from my periphery.

He shrugs and squeezes the steering wheel, laughing softly. "I don't know why I'm nervous, but I am."

Seth's gaze hones in on mine with a glimmering, unspoken misery , and I want to understand what is haunting him. Once we're settled at the hotel, hopefully I can ease whatever is eating at him. Perhaps he'll talk to me.

"Babe, seriously, you've got this. I believe in you!" I reach out and touch his hand, running my fingers up his forearm.

He nods, taking a deep breath and exhaling. "We've got this."

We turn down a long dirt road. Trees stretch toward the sky on both sides of the driveway, heavily laden with green leaves. If it were sunny out, they'd block the sunshine, but it just makes for an eerie, dark passage into the front yard of the inn.

My stomach clenches as I stare out the window. Aside from the untidy landscaping, the plantation house sits in near perfect condition. Yellow paint contrasts with the greenery surrounding the area, and the white trim remains unblemished.

Seth steps out of the car, and I follow suit. He holds his iPhone in his hand, the screen lights up, and he sighs.

"What is it?"

"Go figure, they will be late... Might as well head inside and get started."

His production team is late, but when aren't they? They aren't at the top of my favorite people list, and for many reasons—one of them being laziness. Another is how gross they can be, especially Jimmy. I don't like the way his eyes always linger on me a little too long.

I shudder and study the abandoned inn. Spanish moss hangs from an oak tree, mocking the weeping willow close to it.

Seth has already disappeared from sight. Annoyance ripples through me. I huff and stomp toward the open front door, then more carefully step inside. The last thing I want is to fall through a rotten board.

Inside the house, cobwebs hang from the ceiling and catch the afternoon light just enough to warn me where they are.

Thank God. I hate spiders. I step through the foyer and turn into what I assume is the dining room. To my surprise, it doesn't look half bad. The floorboards are intact, no rot in sight, and although cobwebs hang from the corners and doorways, everything appears in working order.

Half-turning around, I see thick webs near my head and immediately rescind that mental statement, squealing and jumping backward. *Minus* the cobwebs, it isn't half bad, I amend.

I shriek, batting at the webs dangling in front of my face. "Ew! Why, why couldn't you leave trails of gumdrops instead of sticky, horrifying webs?" I shout at the invisible foes lurking in the corners.

Aside from the dust, cobwebs, and faded wallpaper, the house is in perfect condition. No sign of rot or water damage. Curiosity tugs at me, pulling me beyond the dining room and toward a spiral staircase. The banister spins around, stretching toward the second and third floors. God, I would have loved living here when I was little. This place is like a small castle.

The sound of a car door shutting breaks my focus on the banister. A moment later, Seth mutters to himself and his equipment bag thuds on the floor. The last thing I want is to get in his way, so I continue up the stairs, all the way to the third floor.

"Ugh!" I pull at the front of my shirt, willing my core to cool down. Sweat almost instantly coats my skin. The shut windows trap the heat inside, and although it's only June, the warmth in the house is excessive.

The layout is fairly simple. To my left are three rooms. I peek inside each one. Both are fairly simple; a queen-sized bed against the far wall, a dresser against the wall closest to me, and windows to peer out over the property.

On the left side of the hallway are two bedrooms that mirror the others, but one particular door gives me a hard time. The knob twists back and forth, but nothing happens. I wonder if it's locked, or jammed? I grunt as my shoulder connects with the door, and I use the momentum to shove it open.

Half-stumbling inside the room, I quickly assess my surroundings, and spot old wooden blocks stacked against the wall. A rocking horse covered in cobwebs lies on its side and an old, white crib, still dressed for an occupant, faces me from the opposite wall.

A nursery, I muse. It's odd they'd retain a nursery throughout the years. Perhaps they once used the room for the guest's children. On the far wall hangs an aged photograph of a little boy near a pond. His hair is cropped short, allowing me to gaze into his large, almond eyes. He's beautiful, whoever he is.

I kneel and pick up a block, running my fingers along the smoothed over wood. I wonder how many hands played with these? Sighing, I turn my attention to the rocking horse. The yarn mane has long since matted from humidity and cobwebs, but the paint has chipped none. The horse's bay coloring is still intact, as is the white star, however, I curl my lip when I think of how many mice have been in and out of those strands.

Behind the rocking horse, a round knob juts out on a part of the wall, catching my attention. *Curious.* I crawl toward it and tug open the door. As I duck my head, I scan the crawl space for any offending creatures, whether they be rats or evil spiders. I gag immediately. Cobwebs hang low, but I grab an old teddy bear and use it to disperse the webs. As soon as they're gone, I drop the bear and squeal in disgust.

Several boxes line the floor, and on top of one is a newspaper dating back to the early 1900s. A faded picture of a youthful man with long hair and coppery skin looks up at me, but his features are hidden beneath a wide-brimmed hat. Two long braids dangle down his shoulders, and over the jacket he wears.

"That's cool," I mutter.

Another box is full of clothes, and as I rifle through them, most are a small child's. My fingers linger on a stained flower dress and I pick it up. I've always wanted children of my own, but the plan was to wait until I finished college. That was years ago. Every time I mention something to Seth, he changes the subject. Could that be why a rift has steadily grown between us? If he doesn't want children that's fine, but I need to understand so I can move on with my life. That seems to be a theme as of late, avoiding and prolonging the inevitable.

My eyes slide shut, fingers clinging to the dingy dress. I remember the few pregnancy scares we've had over the years, and how relieved Seth was, in contrast to my disappointment. Shaking my head, I clear the memories away.

The nursery door creaks and I freeze. Did Seth already make it upstairs?

A moment ticks by. I strain to listen, but no, I would have heard his heavy footfall. Spinning, I keep my head down and scurry out of the crawl space. Nothing is there, except for a faint shadow that moves over the floor. It grows closer to me, then stops. Fear paralyzes me. I'm unable to tilt my head back, because if I see some ghoulish figure staring back at me, I think I'll expire on the spot.

A cool breeze tickles across my neck and cheek in a soft caress. The shadow pools around my kneeling figure, but somehow I'm not shaking or on the verge of tears like I thought I'd be. The presence doesn't seem malevolent, because anxiety doesn't spread through me like a wildfire. Instead, calm reassurance floods my body, settling whatever fear rises. The sensation is almost like fingertips beneath my chin, but when my head tilts to peer up, the shadow fades and nothing is there.

Good gravy. This place *is* haunted.

2

Whatever touched me in the nursery didn't mean any harm, but it still charges me with enough energy to get the hell out of there and downstairs. Maybe I can convince Seth to venture upstairs. I bet he'd catch high readings.

At the bottom of the stairwell, Seth is talking. His show voice booms loudly, showing far more enthusiasm than I've heard in weeks. Trav is walking around with him, so is the minimal film crew. Seth has a meter in his grasp, reading the room for paranormal activity, and I do my best to stay out of the way. Small beeps ping off the walls, detecting a supernatural presence.

When they spin around, I dodge out of the camera's view and hide in the nook by the stairs. They don't stop to glance at me, instead continue up the stairs where the readings crackle to life.

"There's a story surrounding this house," Seth says. "Once, it was a cotton plantation, but during the war soldiers would come here for food, rest, wound treatment, or to die here. After the war, the owners wanted no part of the house. They said evil lived in the walls. Not to mention they went bankrupt." Seth pauses dramatically as the equipment screeches. "Wow. Not keen on the story?" he asks no one in particular.

"Anyway. The house passed through a few hands over the years, and in 1902, it fell into the possession of Anita Wells. She took orphans in and raised them. In her will, she left everything to a boy she cared for. No one knows his full name, just that his last name was Rainwater. Years later, someone murdered him one night in his sleep. Why? It was never uncovered, but the house passed into another's hands, and from there it became a bed and breakfast. Some say Rainwater still lurks around, too."

Seth always studies the places he ends up going to, so I shouldn't be surprised, but I am. The house itself is a mystery, and something about Rainwater's story makes my heart ache. I glance around the stairwell, wondering how many people this place has housed. Frowning, I think of the boy who inherited it all, only to lose it several years later. How was his murder never solved?

I need air.

Above me, their conversation turns friendly, losing its showy, over-the-top sound. I wonder if they've paused filming for a moment. "Seth, babe, I'm going outside!" If not, they can edit my voice out. I cringe.

Nothing.

Annoyance ripples through me. "Seth!" I grind out this time.

"See that?" Trav shouts. "Turn the camera on again."

Anger tears through me. I'm so tired of being ignored. "I hope I fuck up your filming!" I scream, then storm through the kitchen and outside. I'm being dramatic, but I'm minimally owed a grunt of acknowledgment. This is a theme as of late, and I'm just beyond tired of it all.

I need a change of scenery to calm myself down, so I dart through the kitchen and out the door leading me to the backyard.

To my surprise, a pond is there. A wicker table and two chairs sit under an enormous maple tree near the body of water. I kick off my shoes and walk toward the edge. The pond is clean, with a sandy bottom. My toes squelch in the wet sand, which makes me laugh as it oozes between my toes. After a moment, I wade up to my thighs.

This is exactly what I need to clear my head. When I exhale, it relieves some stress, allowing my shoulders to fall forward. Every muscle in my body hurts, and I chalk it up to more stress.

"Hey, why not try out here?" Trav asks loudly.

My head whips around to glance at the kitchen door. Seth stands there, his eyes flicking toward the pond—to me.

"Why would I?" Seth turns around.

"Humor me, okay?" Trav skulks toward the pond, the device in his hand, and he points it at the water.

Loud beeps hold my attention, but the movement from the corner of my eye steals it. Seth is angrily marching up to Trav.

"Stop it." Seth seethes, but fear swirls in his gaze.

What is he afraid of? I peer down into the water and wonder what he isn't saying. At the same time I'm questioning this, tiny fish weave in and out of my legs. Their dancing urges me to move away, because I imagine them as tentacles, and something sinister. But when I go to shift, something curls around my ankle tightly. A scream lodges itself in my throat.

No sound escapes me, but something pushes against my side, which dislodges me. I stumble on the embankment, looking around, hoping to catch whoever—or whatever—that was.

Seth is unsurprisingly oblivious to my plight.

"Not funny. If that's one of your stupid cameramen, Seth!" I huff.

His gaze lingers on me, then he shakes his head and storms off.

Curses fly free from his mouth. Trav barks at him to calm down, but Seth is stomping off toward the front of the house. I grimace and follow him, because if I don't, I'll be stranded here.

I run up the tiny hill, toward the parking lot, and hurriedly slide into the passenger seat before Seth even has the chance to open his door. When he does, he stares at my soaked body and pinches the bridge of his nose.

"Coming here was an awful idea," he says, gripping the steering wheel tightly.

"Babe, you didn't know how oppressive the energy would be, so don't blame yourself. I didn't know any of that about the house. All the history inside that building... pretty insane."

The strange thing about his reaction is, I didn't feel any oppressive energy, but the look in Seth's eyes tells me he thinks differently. The skin around his eyes is tight, and his eyebrows pitch inward just a little, which only happens when he's anxious.

"No wonder no one wants to buy the house or live inside for long. There is so much darkness surrounding the house, I don't need my sensors for that." Seth pauses to exhale a shaky breath. "I should cut the trip short." He starts the car and pulls out of the driveway.

I know better than to answer him; it was rhetorical, and no matter how much of an argument I put up, it's ultimately his decision. On some of their filming trips, the guys came across buildings causing physical illness. Seth told me he'd wake up, unable to catch his breath, as if someone was suffocating him. Others, it was like his mind was being toyed with. Grim thoughts intruded, plaguing him with depression. I trusted his intuition when it came to leaving a place.

I'm compelled to glance back at the front porch of the house. My heart leaps as I see a shadowy figure leaning against the railing. All I can discern is they're tall and wearing dark clothes, blending into the dim lighting of the porch. With a galloping heart, I turn around in my seat and wonder, *Is that the same apparition from the nursery?*

Instead of returning to the inn the next day, Seth takes two days to gather himself and, as he says, to "cleanse his body and mind." I can't say I blame him, I've seen the aftermath of a particular hard building. He's still jumpy, his blue eyes are bloodshot, and beneath his eyes hang purple bags.

Half-asleep on the bed, Seth curls his arms around me, burying his face in the crook of my neck. "Do I have to go today?" he murmurs in my ear, squeezing me tighter.

"You don't have to do anything.... Unless that anything is *me*." I nudge him with my bottom and laugh.

To my delight, things seem to be returning to normal,

despite my outburst a few days ago. I think my decision to join him down here was the right one.

After we get dressed, we're back on the road to Green Meadow Inn. Seth's demeanor visibly changes as we near the house again. His easy going attitude shifts, and tension etches itself on his face as he works his jaw continuously.

The sun is out in full force, bringing the heat with it. As much as I dislike it, the glow of the sun casts a fresh light on Green Meadow Inn. The yellow paint seems brighter, lending it a hopeful glow. The peonies along the front porch bloomed in the early morning, offering hues of pink to contrast with the white trim. Two days ago, I was too busy to note the beautiful flowers surrounding the house, and now that's all I seem to see.

I wonder, what did this house offer to those in need? What did they think of it as they walked to the front steps, desperate and in search of answers or help?

Seth parks the car and abruptly exits. He's withdrawing from me already. I sit quietly and watch him mill around outside the house, muttering to himself. Not ten minutes later, the rest of the crew shows up, which means I need to make myself scarce.

They're heading back inside, so I venture around the back toward the pond to investigate. I walk toward the embank-ment where I crawled out and squint into the water. There doesn't seem to be a lot of scum, or even twisted branches that could have ensnared me. Perhaps Seth is right, and there is a malevolent presence lurking not only in the water, but also in the house.

"I'm not scared of you," I whisper harshly.

Yet I'm still drawn to the depths, as if something is calling to me, capturing my body and soul. With a splash, I fall in, head first.

Invisible tentacles wrap around my arms, legs, and head, holding me hostage beneath the water. As much as I flail, I can't free myself, and I can't surface to scream. I kick, thrash, and pull toward the surface, but with no luck.

When my hope of breaking free vanishes, and I realize I'm going to drown, that's when I feel arms wrap around my waist, yanking me free. I gasp for breath, gobbling air. Sputtering, I claw at whoever is holding me. Did Seth finally notice I left?

I open my eyes to find a pair of luminous black eyes staring at me. This isn't Seth. I don't know who this man is, but his chiseled jaw leads to a pair of full lips pressed in a grim line. Dark, unbound hair tumbles over his shoulders, contrasting with the white t-shirt.

"I've got you," he says in a husky voice.

As my eyes focus better, I take in the man's appearance with an assessing once-over. His hair is as black as a raven's feather, and it's long—longer than my dark brown waves. His skin is gorgeous; a flawless caramel. I register what he says and promptly remember he's cradling me in his arms.

"T-thank you," I whisper. The shock slowly slips away. Moments ago, I was dragged under the water by something, and nearly drowned. "I don't... I don't know what happened, it was like something drew me in, then kept me under. It wouldn't let go." I sound hysterical, even to myself.

"You're okay, I promise." He places me down in a wicker chair and stands off to the side. "Are you here alone?" His dark eyes sweep the immediate area before he turns back to me.

"No, my boyfriend is inside with his crew."

"Ahmm," he hums, then a lone eyebrow lifts in question. "A crew?"

My hair falls into my line of vision, blocking me from staring at the tall stranger. "Seth, my boyfriend, he films ghost hunting adventures."

"Uh-huh." The handsome man's expression takes on a pinched appearance, lending him a mildly annoyed look. "I see."

"It sounds weird, but..." Does he not believe in ghosts? Not everyone does, which is fine, but it's difficult to know what someone will find offense with these days. Perhaps he doesn't believe in the afterlife.

He smiles, which shifts the ominous clouds from his visage. It instantly warms his face, and his teeth, dear heavens, are so white!

"Hardly. People have always been fascinated with the dead—or demons. It isn't always wise to poke around, though." Tall, dark, and handsome motions toward the house. "We should get you inside. There are towels in the house."

"Crap." My hand flies to my forehead, which still has a steady stream of water pouring down it. This is the second time I've been to this place, and the second time I've been soaked to the bone. "Yes. Wait! How do you know there are towels inside?" I scrunch my nose, grasping my hair to squeeze the water out.

"I take care of the house."

His answers soothe my curiosity, allowing my mind to travel down another pathway. I'm not dead, so how long have I been out here already? Seth must be looking for me.

The chair tumbles to the ground as I stand. My head

nearly collides with the man's chin as he leans over me. "Thank you...?"

He quickly withdraws, so I don't whack my head against him. "Jonathan is the name, and don't thank me...?" His voice pitches lower as he draws his words out, mimicking me. A playful smile tilts the corners of his lips up as he extends his hand toward me in greeting.

I chance another look in his direction, then accept his hand. "Abigail. My name, I mean, my name is Abigail," I stammer, showcasing how awkward I am, and likely always will be.

A door slams in the distance, echoing off the house, and snapping my attention to it. "I'm sorry. I have to go, thank you!" Panic grabs my attention toward the side yard, and I run as fast as I can, leaving Jonathan in my wake.

3

Around the house, the sound of starting engines echoes off the trees. Seth wouldn't leave without me, but a gnawing sensation in my gut tells me otherwise. I'm not a paranoid person. Anxious, but it's not until recently I've started doubting everything I know.

Honestly, I don't know if he *would* leave me behind. The worst feeling in a relationship is not knowing where you stand. During certain moments, I feel like I'm the priority, but the next, it's as if I don't exist at all.

I round the corner of the house, standing next to a purple rose bush, and voices rise in the driveway.

"Just forget her, man, leave her behind."

Trav's voice carries to me, which means his irritating tone is loud enough to carry to Jonathan. My cheeks burn a deep red from embarrassment, only adding to my misery.

"You have your entire life ahead of you, and you're going to waste it on her? You're an idiot."

"Yeah... I'm not agreeing with you, but it's time to find someone else."

"All right. Let's head out, Seth. Just leave Abs behind," Trav says lightly.

He says the words so casually, which hurts the most. Both of them are speaking nonchalantly, as if this isn't my choice, too. I clutch my heart, which seems like it's crumbling inside my chest. Is it possible to die from a broken heart?

I stumble toward the driveway, but I'm too late. The Corolla disappears down the driveway, and with it, my heart vanishes.

A cloud of dust kicks up behind the car, adding insult to injury as it washes over me, sticking to my wet skin.

"What the hell?" I sit on the grass, burying my face into my palms.

Things weren't in the best shape with Seth, but for him to leave, and for Trav to cheer him on without Seth even trying to stick up for me?

I swipe at the tears spilling down my cheek, gulping down air. Something shifts behind me, then a strong, calming presence settles down next to me. Jonathan sits on the grass by my feet.

"Was that him?" Jonathan asks carefully.

"It was," I mumble. It's all I can manage without sounding like a sobbing child. "Why would he leave like that? Why?" Self-loathing settles in, accompanied by self-pity.

Jonathan inches closer to me and wraps an arm around me in a half-hug. "I can't speak for his actions, Abigail. All I can say is, let out whatever is hurting you. Let it out and when you're ready, let it go."

I lean against Jonathan's chest, pressing my cheek against the denim jacket. Beneath it, his body is what I assume a wall of muscle would be like. At this moment, I feel like a complete fool. But he is there, offering comfort as I struggle to breathe through my sobs.

His hand strokes my nape, then swoops down my back. He continues this soothing motion until my breathing calms.

"Sometimes it is best to move on," he says after a few moments roll by. "It isn't easy, but it is necessary for anyone's sanity." Jonathan glances down at me as I pull away.

In my right mind, I'd agree with him, but I'm an emotional wreck and I can't wrap my head around why Seth would be okay just *leaving* me like that. I'll need to call a cab and ride back to Virginia. I'll have to pack all my belongings. The list goes on, making it hard for me to focus, and it upsets me all over.

"I should, but it's hard after five years together. Something has been off for a while, but I wasn't even worth a proper goodbye?" My voice hitches as I fight back stubborn tears.

The inevitable reel of all the things I've done wrong recently plays in my mind. Have I said enough, done enough? Normally, I'm not so clingy, but lately I've felt the need to show I care more, and maybe that made me look desperate.

I hate *feeling* desperate. I'm sure I looked it, too.

"You're still soaked, Abigail. Why don't we get you sorted?" Jonathan stands, extending his hand toward me. "There are towels and I'm sure there is also a change of clothes inside."

Curiosity creeps to the forefront of my mind. "How do you know that again?" I squint, recalling he mentioned looking after the property, but inside, too? "Inside—like the inn?"

Jonathan's eyebrows arch, and he turns to face the house. "Uh, yeah. That would be the one..."

I lift my hands in surrender. "I was just asking... Do you live next door?"

There is no next door. The land belonging to the house is acres wide, and it's probably a decent fifteen minute walk to the next house. I watch as his face slips into an unreadable expression. It's still friendly, but I can't tell if he's laughing at me or not.

"Wait. You live here?"

He chuckles, which makes his full lips twist in a beautiful, toothy smile. "Yes. I realize ghost hunters were just here, but the inn is my home—was—until it sells. I'm not sure you noticed, but there was a *for sale* sign at the bottom of the drive." Jonathan sighs, looking around the yard as if envisioning his childhood. "There is a lot of history in this place. I was born right here."

For a moment my mind lags, then catches up. Jonathan was born here, as in, inside the house. My mouth hangs open for a split second before I snap it shut. I groan at my stupidity. Between stammering and acting utterly foolish, Jonathan must think I'm dimwitted. I blink, wiping a stubborn tear from my cheek.

Jonathan either doesn't see, or has the good grace not to call attention to my lack of detective skills. He chuckles and jerks his thumb toward the house. "Did you see the room off the parlor? The borning room. Many came into the world in that room, and many have left in it. I always thought of it as a doorway; whether you're stepping into life or stepping out, you have to pass through it." He walks away, then pauses as if he senses I'm not joining him. "Come on, let's get you taken care of."

At that, I follow him inside.

Now I know Jonathan lives here, I see the house with new eyes. That's why it didn't appear abandoned, because it isn't.

Even though the cobwebs are thick in some areas, I have to wonder if it's just because this place is so massive. I can hardly keep up on tidying cobwebs in my house—Seth's house, I amend, and pain shoots through my chest.

I don't want to think about Seth, or how Snuffy will react to me not returning, or how *all my belongings* are still in the house, and I'm hundreds of miles away.

"I can't believe him!" The words burst from my mouth and I clench my hands into fists. I have to say something. My thoughts swirl around in my head, deafening me. Every insecurity I've ever had seems to rise, screaming at me.

Jonathan spins on his heel, staring down at me as if I were an alien. "Really?" he questions, and I don't like his tone.

"Why would I? Should I accept the way he went about the breakup? He's thirty years old. You would think he'd have the decency to break up with me like an adult." My shoulders sag and I curl my arms around my middle. "I hate what he did, and how long we've both prolonged the inevitable."

Understanding flashes in Jonathan's gaze. "Which is normal. No one likes to writhe in pain before being put out of their misery." Quiet spreads between us for a few moments, then he says, "I will grab the change of clothes."

Jonathan leaves me to my miserable thoughts. His footsteps carry him across the floor, and since it's so quiet, the sound of him walking around upstairs seems magnified.

Dust peppers my shoulders as he mills around, and I wonder why Jonathan doesn't tidy the place up better. If the house is for sale, shouldn't someone clean the interior? Or at the very least, freshen the place up a little more? It's not as if leaves clutter the floor, but there could be a massive improvement in upkeep. Like purchasing a vacuum, for starters, and buying stock in paper towels.

Despite the knife-like pain in my chest, I mozy into the kitchen and search for some cleaning supplies. Cleaning always pulls me out of the swamps of sadness. Often, when a client infuriated me at the animal hospital, I took it upon myself to go on bathroom cleaning duty, and dove into wiping down the seating area, the tiles. It was nothing but good for the cleanliness of the hospital, and everyone hated to be on mop duty. Not me. Something positive came from my frustration, and that always lifted my spirits.

Beneath the sink, I find a hand towel and a jug of vinegar. At least the glass will be pristine.

4

By the time Jonathan walks into the dining room, the windows are sparkling and the cobwebs are gone. It took more than a towel; it took courage to wipe them away, cursing loudly, and then praying. Finally, a spastic toss of the towel into the trash bin, and it was done. I'm still shuddering in disgust when I feel someone watching me.

Jonathan stands at the entryway, his black brows lifting in question as he takes in my even more disheveled state.

"I wasn't gone that long," he drawls. "Nevertheless, Abigail, I come bearing gifts." Fresh clothes lay on his upturned palms, and he flourishes a bow. The movement shifts his hair, which cascades down his shoulders in a fluid motion.

I try pushing my own from my face, but it sticks in place. How fair is it I look like someone who has been found on the roadside, and he looks near perfect? Frizzy, chestnut strands tickle my temples as I stare at Jonathan in disbelief.

"I know," I say, motioning to the windows. "I clean when I'm stressed out." Stressed doesn't even describe how I feel.

He nods his head, not saying anything. Jonathan still holds the change of clothes out, waiting for me to take them.

I scoop them up, my skin brushing against his. "Thanks," I murmur and step out of the room, toward the bathroom down the hall.

I turn the light on first, half expecting a demonic spider to jump out at me, but nothing does. Closing the door behind me, I peel off my jeans, which glue themselves to my curves. I've never been *thin*. I've always been shapely, which works to my advantage because my hips are holding up the otherwise big, new sweatpants. I remove my shirt and bra, tugging the T-shirt on over my head. My breasts fit against the front snugly.

I flick my hair out from under the shirt as I leave the bathroom, turning on my heel to search for my savior.

To my surprise, Jonathan stands outside the bathroom. I pull up short to avoid colliding with his chest. His hair now lies in a thick braid over his shoulder, which makes it easier for my eyes to follow along his jawline. A fine layer of stubble shadows his angles, only making them appear sharper, and some part of me wants to feel the tickle against my neck.

"Impressive." Jonathan's eyes remain glued to my face.

"Yeah, okay. Enough out of you." I head back outside to hang my wet clothes on the porch railing.

"You didn't ask what I found impressive." Jonathan's deep voice makes me jump. I didn't expect him to follow me. "But I'll answer, regardless. You're wearing clothes that belong to... Come to think of it, I don't know who." He grins, holding up his hands before continuing. "And you're still beautiful."

Is it just me, or is he talking more? I huff, trying not to blush. I don't want compliments now, but I need them. At the very least, it's a distraction. Speaking of distractions, did he say he didn't know whose clothes these are? He's joking, I hope.

"Thank you." After I'm done hanging my clothes, reality creeps in again. "I need to call a cab and figure out where I'm staying, too. Do you have a phone I can use?" Unfortunately, my cell was in the Corolla.

Jonathan waves his hand above him. "No, we don't have a phone line here, but there are plenty of vacant rooms. Stay the night, if you'd like. Tomorrow is another day, and you look exhausted."

I nod and cross the porch, making myself comfortable on a porch swing. At some point, Jonathan joins me, and we settle into a comfortable conversation. It's like I've known him for years, and it's easier talking to him than it ever has been with Seth.

When the peepers begin their song, Jonathan continues to tell me about the inn, and what it was like growing up here. The sound of his deep baritone lulls me into a restful slumber.

Sunlight touches my face, making me sit up in bed. *Bed?* I don't remember walking to a room. I search around, not recognizing the one I'm in, and hurriedly rush to the door. Opening it, I assess the hallway, which wraps around toward another stairwell, and I realize I'm on the second floor. It takes a minute for me to remember. This was the first room I inspected a few days ago.

Scrubbing the sleep from my eyes, I try to remember last night and all I can recall are the stories Jonathan told me. I fell asleep, which is embarrassing. Grumbling to myself, I venture down the stairs in search of him.

Every twist and turn I make through the house leads to empty spaces. Sighing, I push the kitchen door open and head outside into the warm morning glow. The air is already heavy with moisture, and it's like a wet blanket against my mouth. But the sun casts a golden hue on the land, and it's breathtaking. The pond in the backyard glitters from the light, and something about it calls me to the edge. I blink at the dip in the earth, and my toes hit the sandier mud.

I crouch down, touching the surface, feeling myself being pulled deeper. I don't realize I'm calf deep until something grabs my wrist, yanking me back.

"What?" I yelp and stumble against a firm body.

I twist around to find Jonathan staring down at me. At the corner of his almond-shaped eyes, crows feet form, lending warmth to his stony features. His nose twitches as he smiles, showing off his pearly whites.

"I think you should stay away from the water, Abigail." Although his voice comes softly, I hear it for what it is: a warning.

My skin prickles. Despite Jonathan's hold on me, I twist and peer down at the water. There it is again, the strange pull. Fingers dig into my hips and I catch myself leaning toward the depths.

"I don't know what's wrong with me," I murmur, closing my eyes.

Jonathan sighs. "A lot has happened in the last few days. Take a deep breath, relax."

He's right. A lot has happened and while he's a stranger to me, outside of our midnight share fest, I am at peace with him. Like some part of me knows who he is, which is ludicrous! I'm a fractious person, and he's so at ease with everything, so it seems his energy is washing over me.

Once the tension eases from me, Jonathan releases his hold and I move up the embankment. I can't just stay here indefinitely. Somehow I have to get back home, collect my belongings, and move on with my life.

"I need to go to the hotel and talk to Seth." Saying it out loud rattles my nerves, but it's what I have to do.

The quiet man behind me sighs. I sense him move up the embankment. "If you must. I'll be here if you need a place to stay. Green Meadow has always been a place for people to land, and to rest."

I need no more encouragement than that. I venture back inside the house and change into the only outfit I possess.

When I step onto the porch, Jonathan is there, leaning against the rail with his hands in his pockets. His eyes aren't looking at me, they're peering down at the purple carnations below the railing.

"I remember when all these flowers were planted. The land was dug up, mulch trucked in, and I wasn't keen on the change, but looking at it now... I realize it was a pleasant change. What started out as unwanted, and maybe even a little ugly, turned into something breathtaking." Jonathan turns his attention toward me, a slight smile tugging at the corner of his eyes. "I wish you luck, Abigail."

I say nothing in return. Instead, I continue walking down the porch and down the long driveway. All the while, Jonathan's gaze is on my back.

Somehow, it seems like weeks ago, not a day ago, that I passed through the idyllic streets. The row of houses after the long driveway are straight out of a story. Each one possesses a picket white fence, with either a kid or a dog bounding around in excitement.

By the time I reach the gas station, the sun has lost its strength and is dipping down. The hotel wasn't far from here; I remember that. I keep walking until I see the sign.

Immediately, emotions rush toward me, filling me with anxiety.

Inside, the hotel is cool, soothing my heated skin. I advance on the concierge's desk, mustering a smile. "Good evening. I was wondering if room 202 checked out already."

"I'm sorry, I can't share that information with you."

"He's my fiancé. Seth Rogerson is staying in 202."

"Oh, okay. Let me see." She dips her head down, typing something into her computer. "Ah, okay. He just checked out."

I groan. "Thanks. I'm surprising him while he's down here working." Gathering humor I don't feel, I laugh and bring my palm to my forehead. "Time to catch him!"

Quickly, I walk outside and stand on the curb, assessing the parking lot. A Corolla pulls out of its space and comes toward the curb where I am. To my surprise, it's Seth.

My confidence falters as Seth turns his gaze in my direction. His head jerks away from me, then back again, but instead of surprise on his face, it's panic—and something else. His fingers grip the steering wheel as he stomps on the breaks. The mixed emotions on his face trickle to his jaw, and he clenches it.

"Why are you doing this?" he shouts, pounding the wheel.

Why am I doing this? I glare at him, stomping toward his car. Seth's eyes close, he shakes his head and swallows roughly.

"Because you left me without a word?"

"Whatever you want to believe, understand that I loved you more than life, Abigail. But it's time to move on." He shakes his head and pulls out of the parking lot, leaving me for the second time in two days.

This isn't how it's supposed to end.

5

It's difficult to sift through my emotions, but anger is just around the corner. It creeps into my chest, and as luck would have it, the sky darkens on my way back to the inn, and it downpours.

When I arrive in the parking area, I'm as soaked as I was from my near drowning experience. I stop in my tracks, focusing on a dark figure on the porch—Jonathan. He stands hunched over the rail, forearms resting against it, his gaze on me, but no trace of a smile. Whatever he sees on my face brings him off the deck and toward me. His arms encircle my form and his lips brush a kiss against my head.

"If this will be a theme, tell me now, and I'll get some extra clothes for you."

I laugh against his solid frame, tears mixing with the rain cascading down my cheeks. "I don't know if I should trust your sense of style."

My statement earns me a raised brow in response. Nothing is wrong with Jonathan's style. He's wearing a form fitted t-shirt today, which showcases his firm chest and solid arms. The jeans he has on are a looser fit, but something tells me his legs are as muscled as the rest of him.

"Abigail—"

"Do you think—" We start at the same time, but when he pauses and nods his head, I continue. "Do you think I could stay here for two weeks? I have it off work, anyway. I'm not ready to go home… Or, rather, return to the shambles of my life."

Jonathan brushes a piece of wet hair from my face and tucks it behind my ear. "As long as you want to stay here, Abigail, you have a place at Green Meadow." His gaze lifts toward the sky and he chuckles. "But maybe we should head inside."

The rain continues to pelt us, and it doesn't take long for him to become as wet as I am. Perhaps I'm finally losing it, or it's the fact I'm set free from a dying relationship, but amidst my tears I laugh and grab Jonathan by the hands.

"Will you dance with me?" I blurt, hoping like the fool I am that he says yes.

At first, he doesn't speak, then he moves closer and slides his arm around my waist. Carefully, he takes my hand in his. "Yes, I reckon I will."

And so we slow dance in the pouring rain, with lightning flashing around us, and the thunder rolling.

Water drips from Jonathan's lashes as he stares down at me. He gives me a lopsided grin, and he breaks our comfortable silence by speaking. "We should head in."

He's right, the rain is coming down in sheets, and the thunder is growing louder. In a blink, he scoops me up in his arms and dodges up the stairs, darting into the house. He's laughing, and it's not the chuckle I've grown used to, but a louder, playful sound.

Jonathan doesn't stop as he slides into the house. His large frame skates across the hardwood floor and his shoulder stops his momentum as he collides into the wall. Reluctantly, he releases me and I slip to the floor.

We're both still laughing and looking like half drowned cats.

A wild grin pulls at his lips, and those beautiful teeth flash against his dark skin. He's gorgeous. At this moment, with his hair slicked against his face and wildness in his gaze, I'm drawn to him. I shouldn't be, because I've known him for exactly three days, and yet I learned more about him in that time span than I ever did with Seth in five years.

We're still close enough that his hair drips onto my upturned face. I lift myself up on my tiptoes, then pull on the front of his shirt. My eyes shouldn't be open, but I wonder at the last minute if I'm reading the situation right. He leans in halfway. I can almost taste his lips against mine, but he stops just short of meeting me.

Jonathan's hands cup my cheeks, and he shakes his head. "Not like this. Allow yourself to heal, and then we'll see what happens."

Fair enough, but it feels like someone's slapping my hand for sticking it in the cookie jar. I step backward, putting more distance between us than necessary, and the silly moment turns into an awkward one.

"I'm going to change—again." I point toward the stairs and promptly run up them.

Once I'm in comfortable, dry clothing, I collapse on the bed I claimed as mine. As I stare up at the ceiling, I can't seem to cry, or find anything other than anger in my heart. It's finally time to let go of Seth, and that's exactly what I plan to do.

Over the next week, Jonathan surprises me with an extra set of clothes, minus panties and a bra. While it isn't an outfit I'd rave about, it's something. I laugh at the screen-printed tee that reads *Mud and Mascara*, which oddly seems to fit the state I constantly find myself in. The jeans are a duplicate pair of the ones I already have, meaning he purposely inspected them.

On my last day in Russell, South Carolina, I lounge on the porch swing with Jonathan. How was it already time to leave? The days have dragged on slowly, giving the illusion I've been here a lifetime. I lean against Jonathan's shoulder, and his arm wraps around me instinctively.

Tomorrow, I'll be leaving. Not just the inn, or South Carolina, but Jonathan, too. Something about that doesn't sit well with me.

"What happens when I go home?" I turn, looking up at his sharp nose.

"What do you want to happen?" he asks, staring down at me with his unreadable expression.

What I want is foolish. I want to stay, to learn more about Jonathan, and explore what could happen between us—if anything. But there's a life back at home waiting for me, too. My job. My cat. My family.

Jonathan's fingers slide along my jaw, up into my hairline, then he taps on my forehead. "Always thinking, but never speaking." He smiles as he withdraws his hand.

I'm a terrible speaker. Not just in public, but I have issues voicing my thoughts and opinions, so he isn't wrong, and I'm not offended. But I'm also tired of just talking and not acting.

I can't stand the idea of returning home and never experiencing what it's like to kiss Jonathan. Without thinking, without speaking, I lean forward and capture his lips between mine. At first Jonathan tenses, then his arms envelop my waist, and he tugs me into his lap. I straddle him as I deepen the kiss, my tongue sliding against his in a sensual, slow dance.

Jonathan tips his head back, his long hair cascading over the bank of the swing as we savor one another. He groans into my mouth, then shifts beneath me. I can feel him straining against his pants, heating my core further. Desire unfurls in my belly, spreading like wildfire through my veins. I want to explore every inch of him and soothe the yearning tearing through me.

It's reckless and stupid, but this is what I crave more than anything right now. Judging by Jonathan's response, I think it's what he wants, too. I rock my hips against him, and in return he sucks in a breath.

His arms tighten around my waist, then in a quick movement, he stands up and walks us into the house. He hesitates for a moment, then turns into the living room and lays me down on the oversized couch.

Jonathan peels his shirt from his body and tosses it aside. I swallow roughly and lean up, letting my fingers trace along the ridges of his abs; muscle lays over muscle. I hesitate over raised scars, tracing them in a feather light touch. *Who would do this to him?* Who would hurt this gentle, beautiful man?

Jonathan reaches out and his hands cup my face tenderly, drawing my attention away from the scars. His lips begin a slow dance with mine, and every piece of me aches as he draws it out.

"Please," I murmur. I don't want teasing kisses or touches, only the physical contact my body desperately yearns for.

He hesitates for a moment, as if wondering if he should continue his delicious torture, but in a blink, he peels away my shirt and bra. Each touch, each kiss is warm and exquisitely slow. Jonathan's full lips trail down my belly, and he slips my pants and underwear off.

I'm naked before him, my bodily imperfections on display, but his eyes are open and full of hunger. I lean forward, undoing his jeans and pushing them down his slender hips.

"I don't want to forget this," I whisper against his lips.

"I'll do my best to ensure you don't." His laughter rumbles in his chest, then Jonathan makes good on his promise. Imprinting himself on my body and mind.

After, Jonathan carries me up to his room, and curls his arms around me, pulling me against his chest. For the second time, I fall asleep against his warm body. As my consciousness tumbles into darkness, all I can think of is this moment, Jonathan's crooked smiles, and his husky voice.

When I wake next, he's nowhere to be found. I quickly dress, then wander around downstairs in search of him. A thud upstairs on the third floor catches my attention, and I jog up the spiral staircase. After two weeks of being here, I know where all the rooms are, and head toward the sound. I'm feeling a little frisky and maybe he's ready for a second round already, too.

Except, when I make it to the doorway of the room he's in, the sight of his naked torso makes me pause. Light filters in through the window, passing straight through his scarred chest, and the wall-length mirror he stands in front of shows no reflection. I swallow roughly and stumble back, my foot catching on a raised floor board.

Falling backward, I crash into the wall. My heart thunders away as I piece everything together. How Jonathan always seemed to show up out of nowhere, how he was always there when I needed him.

Jonathan turns around, his ebony hair framing his face. Mixed emotions flicker in his gaze, and I have trouble deciphering them. Surprise, guilt? He holds his hands by his side as he approaches me, slowly, like I'm a cornered wild animal liable to run away. I *want* to run away.

"I can explain," he begins.

I laugh. My hands cover my eyes and as I pull them away, they are coated in salty tears. "I've lost it," I murmur, shaking my head. "You're not real."

But last night... I felt him, my body *still* aches from our actions.

"No, you haven't, Abigail. I promise I am real." Jonathan crosses the distance between us, but I step away from him, shaking my head in disbelief again. "Will you listen to me?" He lifts a hand upward, approaching me slowly. "Please?" he asks quietly.

Hysteria blooms in my mind. A smile tickles my lips, and I wave my hands toward his still bare torso. "Go ahead."

But I wonder, is Jonathan a figment of my broken mind? I'm no stranger to mental health, I've had my fair share of panic attacks, but I've never hallucinated before. I frown, rubbing my temples as I sort through my recent memories. Could I have imagined him in my loneliness?

"Abigail," Jonathan says, snapping me from the dark rabbit hole I started down. "You're not seeing things. I'm not... of this world anymore, but neither am I a part of the afterlife. Some people call us revenants, others ghosts. I can become as real as the house, as anyone else. I can touch, you can feel me, but I can also fade to nothing."

"Like Casper?"

Jonathan squints as me, as if trying to figure out who Casper is. "I don't know who that is."

"He's a friendly cartoon ghost." I cover my lips with my fist, realizing how stupid I sound.

"Maybe?" Jonathan stares at me, confusion still crinkling his forehead.

Casper doesn't look like Jonathan, not in ghost form or human form. Devon Sawa is pale, has blond hair and blue eyes, and was gorgeous to my ten-year-old self. I remember watching the movie when I was little and wishing to high heavens that he'd remain alive, and human, to stay with Kat. Selfishly, I wanted them to have a happily ever after, but those don't always exist in the real world.

Maybe this is a dream. That would explain the similarities between Casper and whatever *this* is.

Jonathan lifts his hand and touches my cheek. I jump in response and he reluctantly pulls away. "I didn't tell you, because I didn't think you'd stay this long. I thought you'd leave and forget me."

"Forget you?" I echo. "I couldn't forget you."

I drag my gaze from his scarred chest to his eyes. They're full of a deep sadness that makes my heart clench and ache. Death may separate us, but what we experienced earlier was something. I believe in ghosts as much as I believe in wearing white after labor day.

Something clicks in my head. "Was that you... in the nursery?"

Jonathan reaches forward, and this time I allow his hand to continue moving. His fingers brush along the side of my neck, up my cheek, and the motion is so feather-light, I close my eyes.

"It was. Every time you were alone, every time you'd break down, I was there, trying to comfort you."

As he speaks, recent memories of the past two weeks filter through my mind. In the nursery I felt him, in the kitchen while I choked on a sob his presence was there behind me. Even before I met him, I knew him in some manner, which would explain why the connection was so easily made.

"Are you all right?"

"... Yes. I think—I think I'd like to stay for a few more days."

Jonathan dips his head down, brushing his lips against my temple. "You can stay as long as you'd like, and if forever's how long you wish to stay, then forever I'll keep you."

How does he know what to say at exactly the right time?

My hands rest against his chest, and I can feel the scars beneath the shirt. "Now that I know, can you tell me what happened—the entire story?"

He nods, but withdraws from me as he turns toward the nursery. "You saw something when you were here."

He crosses toward the crawl space and opens the door. Reaching for something, he pulls out a newspaper and hands it to me. "That's me. The reason Seth's sensors went off when he spoke about Rainwater, it's because *I am* Rainwater."

My eyes fall to the paper I remember from two weeks ago. The shadowy figure hidden beneath a wide-brimmed hat. Braids tumble over the man's shoulders, but I don't have to see the face now to realize who it is. It's Jonathan. Jonathan Rainwater, the young man who was murdered in this house almost a hundred years ago.

"Now you know the missing pieces. Why they did it, I don't understand. No one ever looked into it, and the house promptly went on the market again. It's passed through several hands, but no one has ever stayed." He pauses, grinning. "Maybe I'm a poor house guest."

I can easily guess why someone would do it. Prejudice back then was far more vicious than it is now, but my heart breaks for him. But I doubt that he's a rude resident.

"Oh, Jonathan," I murmur, dropping the newspaper. "I'm sorry."

A sad smile touches his lips, but not his eyes. "It was long ago." Moving around me, he exits the room and sighs.

I follow him, then take his hand and lead him down to his bedroom. Pushing him into the sunlit room, I quickly remove his shirt, and make love to him until the sadness washes away from his expression.

6

Reluctantly, I wake. Jonathan's arms wrap around me, his chin resting against my shoulder. His body against mine comforts me in a way I desperately need. I can't speak—can't move. I'm trapped in an in-between state where dreams, or perhaps distant memories, dance before me. Blurry faces bob in my mind's eye, but no voices accompany them. The sensation of phantom touches coats my body in goosebumps, as well as a cold sweat.

The impression of hands against my body sends chills throughout, because Jonathan is still, and he isn't moving. Which means the touches I feel *are* in my head, but the foreign, unknown touch is a caress, and my anxiety eases. It's a strange pull, tempting me to move from the bed, but Jonathan's presence is enough to cement me in place.

When he wakes, he brushes the hair off my neck. Tension oozes from me, but as his lips leave a trail of kisses beneath my ear, he whispers softly, "Come back to me, Abigail." How can he know I'm slipping away? "I'm here, Just come back to me." His arm tugs me closer to his frame, then his nose buries into my neck. "Don't leave."

The images flicker violently in my head, but Jonathan's

words trickle into my mind, and I focus on them. On the way his body feels against mine, and how he sounds so utterly broken.

"Come back," he repeats, his voice cracking.

His tone undoes whatever is holding me prisoner. I lift my hand, letting my fingers graze his forearm. Jonathan raises his head, squeezing me tightly.

"I'm okay," I say. "It was just a weird dream."

But was it? Or was it something else? It's similar to the same pull from the pond. The all-encompassing dread, the feeling of plummeting into a darkness that will consume me until I'm nothing more.

Jonathan says nothing in response. Does he sense something off, I wonder, or were his words directed toward the fact I'll be leaving soon?

Slowly, I sit up and run my hands over my face. They're trembling, but Jonathan is there, as he has been since I arrived. My heart twists, because I realize then I'm falling for a ghost—a man who isn't even alive.

His hair tumbles over his bare chest in a tangled mess, his somber gaze focused wholly on me. So intense, so full of anguish. I lean over toward him and trace his full lips with my thumb.

"I'm here. I don't plan on going anywhere." The words slip from me, surprising me, and even him.

"Is that so?" Jonathan's lips shift into a slight smirk. "Can you promise that?" He moves so quickly I don't have the chance to move away. His arms encircle me again, holding me hostage in his lap. "I'll hold you to it, Abigail," he purrs my name.

"If it's anything like this, I'm okay with that." I laugh,

which quickly turns into a gasp as he shifts beneath me. The mood lightens as desire spreads between the two of us, and it draws my eyes to his bottomless pools of black. "I think..." I whisper. "I love you."

Jonathan's gaze remains shuttered until I speak. "I don't have to think about that." He leans in, kisses the column of my throat and then moves to my ear. "I've loved you since you stumbled into my life." Jonathan chuckles, slipping a hand against my cheek. "If you want to call my existence a life."

Jonathan shifts under me, against my skin, and I gasp. Anyone that can make me feel as he does, anyone that can pull me back from the oblivion that continuously threatens to pull me under, is viable. "You are more alive than most, Jonathan."

He pulls me flush against his chest, bringing forth a moan from me, then he spends the rest of the morning showing me how alive he is—we are—until we are thoroughly exhausted.

The days fly by, much to my dismay. Each day, Jonathan grows quieter, his eyes more watchful, and it fills me with anxiety. What is he waiting for? Me to leave, me to stay?

Except today. I can't find him anywhere in the house. So I venture outside, hoping to discover where he's hiding.

He's not on the porch swing, nor milling around the yard like he usually is, and he's not in the backyard.

I pause next to the pond, eyeing it with trepidation. Is there some force beneath the surface, some demon trying to trap me? Images flutter behind my eyes, similar to the other day.

My hands rush to my throat as panic fills me out of nowhere. I can't breathe. I want to scream, but when I do, I cough up water. Violent retches shake my body, driving me to my knees, and somehow I'm already in the pond.

Water encompasses my body, filling every one of my senses. I'm trying to break loose from whatever has me in its clutches, thrashing violently against its hold. Jonathan isn't here to save me, and this time I'm going to die.

Blackness fills my vision, and my body floats. Despite water pouring into my lungs, I'm conscious—I think. Suspended in the water, memories flash through my mind again, but this time they're clear, as if I'm watching a movie reel.

Seth is inside Green Meadow Inn. His crew for the tv show is late, including his best friend Trav—no shocker there. I feel relieved. I'm hiding inside one of the bathrooms, biting in my bottom lip as I stare down at a pregnancy test. I'm pregnant. Happiness warms every nerve. We hadn't been trying, but we weren't not *trying, either.*

"Baby, you almost done in there?" Seth knocks on the door.

I open it, holding the pee stick as I look at him. "Yes, daddy." I wiggle the stick and his face lights up. In a blink, he's picking me up and swinging me around.

"Really?"

"Yes... I can't fake it." I laugh, slipping down his body and tugging on his hand. "Come on, before the crew gets here."

Seth's eyes flick over my shoulder toward the door. "We have a few minutes if I go by their track record." He kisses me tenderly, then deeply as he holds my face in his grasp. "God, baby... I love you. Us." He drops to his knees and kisses my nonexistent bump, then pulls back.

Giddy, we run outside, stripping our clothes as bolt into the pond. Seth scoops me up, my legs wrapping around him as we celebrate the life we made.

A moment after we've finished, his phone rings. Of course... It's likely his crew interrupting. He winces and pulls away.

"It's fine," I say, half meaning it. When he makes it to the embankment I swim away, then dive deep into the depths of the pond, laughing from the absolute happiness I feel. Bubbles of air escape me, then I feel the familiar press of needing air, so I push myself upward, but I can't move.

My ankle is caught on something. A root of some kind? I bend to loosen it, but it's no good. I can't. Seth should be in soon, he will find me. He has to.

Desperation fills me. I have to pull myself free. I'm panicking because I can't breathe. I'm not ready to die, not when I'm about to have a baby.

No one pulls me from the water. I drown. I'm dead.

Seth dives into the water, pulling my lifeless body free from the roots. He's sobbing over my blue body, cursing himself, his crew. Everyone.

Strong arms yank me out. I gasp, immediately puking up water. "What am I?" I flail in Jonathan's arms. "Tell me, please?"

His mouth parts, but he closes it and removes both of us from the pond. He doesn't speak until we are on the front porch swing. "You are Abigail Reed. But you are not alive and haven't been for three years. Every year you relive your death, then begin it anew. From the few weeks leading up to you leaving Virginia, to your death."

My hands cover my face. "Seth didn't dump me?"

Jonathan carefully pries my hands away, his fingers squeezing them. "No. You died here, in that pond. Every year Seth returns to Green Meadow, hoping to talk to you, and every year you wish to reunite with him. Except... this year has been different."

"Different, how?" My question sounds sharp even to my ears.

Jonathan grimaces at my tone. "I've been a part of this inn for a hundred years, and since the moment you stepped onto the property, I've watched you. Every time your loop begins, I comfort you, and every year you forget me." His dark eyes flick downward, then he shifts uncomfortably. "Didn't you wonder why you were at ease with me? You've known me since your spirit clung to this world. I've never left you." His hands drag down his face as he sighs. "But this year, instead of returning with Seth, you stayed behind, and apparently you were more prepared for the breakup."

This is more than I can comprehend.

"I couldn't watch you do it again. I had to break the cycle, Abigail. Please look at me." He tries to turn my head to look at him, but I pull away, then stand.

I peer down at my hands, fully expecting them to become translucent, like Casper, but they don't. They are still my hands; still appearing to possess life.

"But if I'm dead, the woman at the hotel... She saw me." None of this makes sense.

"You're a revenant, like me. You can flicker in and out of the corporeal form, so when you're upset, you can't control it.

Did you notice Seth reacting to things you said or did? It's because he saw them, heard them." He speaks gently, grimacing as he mentions Seth.

At first, I think my heart races furiously in my chest, but as my hands rest against my breast, nothing beats beneath them. Just in case I'd doubted Jonathan's words, the proof is in the lack of a steady thrum.

Jonathan reaches out to comfort me, but I pull away.

"I need a moment," I say.

The fresh pain from the memories twists my insides. But it's confusion and hurt riding in the front seat. The past few weeks shift around in my mind, holes filling as the truth settles into place. I see everything in a fresh light.

Why Seth ignored me at the house, and Snuffy curled around my legs. Our cat knew I was there, while Seth could feel me whispering across his skin. His attitude toward the brewed coffee cleared. He wasn't agitated because I made it, but because a freaking *ghost* made it.

In rapid succession, every interaction becomes clear, landing me on my bottom. I feel sick, but nothing is in my stomach. A shaky breath escapes me, out of reflex and not necessity.

Jonathan didn't betray me, but he withheld information, and I'm not sure if I'm okay with that. I know I love him, and I know my heart still aches for Seth, but if it's been several years, wouldn't Jonathan try something—anything? Perhaps I'm being too harsh.

9

Silence spreads between me and Jonathan, and as it does, a compartment inside of my mind unlocks. Light spears through my eyes, sending me to the ground again. I gasp as flashbacks trickle in, replacing the old reel with the recent memories. Instead of spending time with Seth, I see Jonathan, comforting me, making me laugh—and not for the first time, my heart twists.

The fog of confusion, accompanied with despair, dissipates. Jonathan is hovering over me, but I don't turn to look at him. I need my space.

"Abi—" My name dies on Jonathan's lips, because I bolt away from him, into the house, and upstairs.

Every year has been the same. I'm forced to relive the wretched memories and experience the loss of what could have been. I can't imagine that it is good for anyone's mental health, including a dead person's.

I groan, flopping onto my bed, then roll over to hug my pillow. Overwhelmed doesn't begin to describe how I feel, and I don't know what to be more upset about—the untruth, or losing my small family? Closing my eyes, I slip into whatever a ghost calls their resting period.

When I wake next, the sun isn't up. Has it been a day, or weeks? I don't know.

I rise from bed and head downstairs. Jonathan is sitting at the dining room table, reading a book. If he notices me, he doesn't show any signs. Annoyance tears through me. How could he withhold the truth?

"Why not tell me sooner?" I ask, an edge to my tone.

He pulls his gaze from his reading, then calmly asks me, "Would it have made a difference?"

The fight evaporates from me. It wouldn't have, and I hate to admit it. So, I don't. "Do you know everything about me?"

"I do. The first year, you broke down and told me all about you. Where you're from, what it was like growing up." Jonathan closes the book and sets it down. He watches as I step further into the dining room.

"And the second year?"

"The second, you wished to stay here at Green Meadow. You didn't, in the end. You went back to Churchville, or at least in your memories you did. It started the entire process again." He frowns as he says this.

My heart aches. "Is that why you clung to me in bed, begging me to come back? You thought it was happening?"

"I knew it would happen soon." His broad shoulders sag, but he stands up and closes the distance separating us. Lifting his hands, he cups my cheeks and holds my gaze. "What will you tell me this year? What words will you give me to cling on to?" Jonathan waits patiently for what I'd say next.

Honestly? With my emotions raw from the events flashing

before my eyes, I want to tell him to let me have a moment. But what I want more is his arms around me.

"I've told you a few things. I love you, for starters..." I hiccup in the middle of a laugh, which turns into crying. "But you won't have to remind me, because this time I'm not leaving. I don't want to go through that every year. It ends here."

Jonathan's black brows knit together. "What do you mean?"

"I'm letting go of my life with Seth. I'm not alive, and I never will be again. You said you'd have me forever if I wish, and that's what I want, Jonathan Rainwater."

Fear blazes in his eyes, and his fingers tense on my skin. Like he's afraid I'll vanish in the next moment.

"Is that a proposal?"

"I reckon," I tease. "Consider it an unromantic proposal by a swamp rat."

He peels away wet strands of hair from my cheeks. A slow, sensuous smile spreads across his face. "Well, Miss Reed, I accept."

Before he has the chance to make the next move, I pull his face toward mine and kiss him slowly.

If this is the way I'm to spend the rest of my days as an apparition, I don't mind at all.

About Elle

Elle was born and raised in Southeastern, Massachusetts in a little farm town by the harbor. She grew up fascinated with all things whimsical and a strong love for animals. As she grew so did her passion for reading and writing. Although she prefers devouring all genres she largely enjoys dark fantasy.

She is married to her best friend and has two lively sprites who inspire madness, love and a sense of humor in her. They also have a menagerie of animals, two dogs, three cats and a horse. In her downtime, Elle enjoys creating candles, crocheting, horseback riding and running.

Dear readers,

Thank you for taking the time to read Midnight Tide's first anthology. We hope you enjoyed reading our unique stories centering around all things spooktacular.

A special thanks goes out to Tanya, thank you for taking the time to read through, and cheer the authors on. You're an amazing individual, and we appreciate your hard work.

—authors of Something in the Shadows Anthology

The Girl in the Clockwork Tower by Lou Wilham

A tale of espionage, lavender hair, and pineapples.

Welcome to Daiwynn where magic is dangerous, but hope is more dangerous still.

For Persinette—a lavender-haired, 24-year-old seer dreaming of adventure and freedom—the steam-powered kingdom of Daiwynn is home. As an Enchanted asset for MOTHER, she aids in Collecting Enchanted and sending them to MOTHER's labor camps.

But when her handler, Gothel, informs Persi that she will be going out into the field for a Collection, she decides it's time to take a stand. Now she must fight her fears and find a way to hide her attempts to aid the Enchanted or risk being sent to the camps herself.

Manu Kelii, Captain of the airship The Defiant Duchess, is 26-years-old and hasn't seen enough excitement—thank you very much. His charismatic smile and flamboyant sense of style earned him a place amongst the Uprising, but his fickle and irresponsible nature has seen to it that their leader doesn't trust him.

Desperate to prove himself, Manu will stop at nothing to aid their mission to overthrow MOTHER and the queen of Daiwynn. So, when the Uprising Leader deposits a small unit of agents on his ship, and tasks him with working side by side with MOTHER asset Persinette to hinder the Collection effort, he finds himself in over his head.

The stakes are high for this unlikely duo. They have only two options; stop MOTHER or thousands more will die— including themselves.

Available
9.23.20

Lyrics & Curses by Candace Robinson

Lark Espinoza could get lost in her music—and she's not so sure anyone in her family would even care to find her. Her trendy, party-loving twin sister and her mother-come-lately Beth, who's suddenly sworn off men and onto homemaking, don't understand her love of cassette tapes, her loathing of the pop scene, or her standoffish personality. For outcast Lark, nothing feels as much like a real home as working at Bubble's Oddities store and trying to attract the attention of the cute guy who works at the Vinyl shop next door—the same one she traded lyrical notes with in class.

Auden Ellis silences the incessant questions in his own head with a steady stream of beats. Despite the unconditional love of his aunt-turned-mother, he can't quit thinking about the loss of his parents—or the possibility he might end up afflicted with his father's issues. Despite his connection with lyric-loving Lark, Auden keeps her at arm's length because letting her in might mean giving her a peek into something dangerous.

When two strangers arrive in town, one carrying a mysterious, dark object and the other playing an eerie flute tune, Lark and Auden find that their painful pasts have enmeshed them in a cursed future. Now, they must come to terms with their budding attraction while helping each other challenge the reflection they see in the mirror. If they fail, they'll be trapped for eternity in a place beyond reality.

Available
11.11.20